IN THE GRASP

LA WOLVES · BOOK ONE

CADENCE KEYS

For my son, who gave me the courage to chase what I thought was an impossible dream.

PART 1: THEN

ONE

Paige

Falling in love with my best friend was never part of the plan.

It feels like I've known Jack my whole life. We first met on the playground at school my first day of kindergarten. I was sitting on the swings, still struggling with that legs-forward-then-kick-back thing to get myself moving—I was mostly just kicking up the wood chips that made up the playground and barely swinging at all. Next thing I know, three first-grade boys came up to me and told me I had to move.

I've never liked being told what to do—I think it comes from having two obnoxious older brothers who always try to boss me around. But who really knows; maybe I'm just stubborn. Basically, I told the boys they could have their pick of the other ten open swings, but they kept hassling me. They started jostling my swing's handles, forcing me to cling to it to keep from being thrown off.

Behind my bullies, I heard a boy shout, "Hey, stop that." The boys parted, and that's when I first laid eyes on Jack Fuller.

He was cute even then, not that I was really paying attention at that point. Boys still had cooties as far as I was concerned.

My bullies didn't like that someone came along to spoil their fun, and they ended up pushing Jack down. He got up and punched the biggest one in the face. The boy promptly burst into tears, and then the whole group ran away. Jack watched them carefully, then he walked up to me, his cute little face frowning, and looked at me closely.

"Are you okay?" he asked.

"Yeah, thanks," I said.

He proceeded to sit in the swing next to me and then spent the remainder of recess teaching me how to properly use my legs to gain momentum. At the end of recess, he told me that I was now his best friend, and he'd always protect me. I thought he was just being nice, but it's been over ten years since that day, and he's still my best friend.

Today is the first day of our junior year at Thomas Aquinas Preparatory School, a private school in Vancouver, Washington that's just right across the river from Portland, where most of us hang out when we're not at school. I haven't seen Jack all summer since he's been at an intensive football camp that only finished a week ago. He's an amazingly talented quarterback, and there have already been several scouts from universities around the nation at his games. I'm beyond proud of him because I know how badly he wants to go pro.

But it's been hard not seeing him this summer. It's the first summer we've gone without seeing each other since we were five years old. We tried to talk on the phone at night when he had some time, but he was usually pretty tired.

Honestly, I've missed him more than I thought I would. I'm sure this will sound crazy since I'm only a sixteen-year-old girl, but I think I'm in love with him. I haven't told him, and I'm pretty sure I've been successful in keeping my feelings to myself since he's given me no hint that he knows. But ever since we entered high school, it's gotten harder to hide how I feel. It's also been harder to pretend I don't notice how attractive Jack's becoming. The way his mesmerizing dark blue eyes light up when he laughs, or how the muscles in his arms have become more prominent due to all his extra time in the gym in an effort to bulk up for football.

It's dangerous feeling this way for my best friend. He's the one person in my life I can always go to and rely on. I tell him everything, but I'm terrified if I tell him how I feel, it could ruin our friendship. On the other hand, there's a possibility he might feel it too, and we could end up dating. My heart speeds up a little at the idea. A third possibility is he could politely reject me but still want to be friends, which would absolutely crush me. The thought of watching Jack date other girls already makes me want to vomit, but if I had to watch him with the knowledge that he knows how I feel, I think I would actually die.

I need to stop thinking about this.

Jack's picking me up in ten minutes to drive me to school, and I'm practically giddy with excitement. It took me forever to figure out which outfit to wear, but I eventually settled on a cute, deep red summer dress with cap sleeves. It accentuates my figure, just like the magazines suggest I should in order to get a boy's attention. It's the first time I've ever taken the advice of a magazine, but I figure they have to know what they're talking about, right? I also put on makeup, using the colors the girl at Sephora advised to bring out the brown in my eyes, while my dark brown hair lies in loose curls just past my shoulders. The chime of the doorbell rings throughout the house just as I finish applying my lip gloss.

"I got it!" I yell as I grab my backpack and run down the stairs.

Swinging open the door, my eyes widen as I absorb the sight before me and fight not to drop my jaw to the ground.

Holy shit. Jack got way hot.

His brown hair is cut short on the sides, a little longer on the top, and looks slightly mussed like he's been running his fingers through it. His deep blue eyes widen as his gaze drops slowly down my body in such a blatant perusal that my heart feels like it might beat right out of my chest. His gaze finally slides back up until he makes eye contact with me, and the smile that covers his face is dazzling.

"Wow, Paige. You look great!"

He steps into the house and wraps his arms around me in a tight hug, making my whole body feel warm and my heart slam against my chest from his proximity. He smells so good. I close my eyes and squeeze him back, convinced this is heaven.

Man, I've got it bad.

He pulls back, not looking nearly as affected as I'm sure I do. "You ready to go?"

"Yep!" I turn around to pull the door closed after we walk out, trying to hide the blush that's spread over my fair cheeks. "Bye, Mom, see you after school." I think she calls back, but I don't hear her before the door closes, and I follow Jack to his BMW 3-series.

Have I mentioned his parents are loaded? Personally, I don't think a sixteen-year-old boy needs a brand-new car, but since it's now my ride too, I guess I can admit it's pretty cool. He opens the door for me, and I slide in. I take a few deep breaths as he walks around the car, hoping I can calm my crazy heartbeat. When he gets in he glances at my legs as he starts the car, and I can feel the blush on my cheeks deepen.

He clears his throat, slides his sunglasses on, and refocuses on the road. "So, how was your summer? We didn't get to talk much while I was at football camp." He glances at me briefly before concentrating on the road.

Are his cheeks turning pink, or am I imagining things?

"It was amazing. I spent some time on my grandparents' farm in Eastern Washington."

"Those are the ones with the horses, right?"

"Yep. My grandpa actually let me name one that they got while I was there. I hated that I had to leave him. I miss him already."

"More than you missed me?" He smiles at me as he says it, and I can feel my blush deepen further. At this rate, my cheeks will be darker than the red of my dress before we even make it to school. I really need to get myself under control. It's never been this hard to hide my feelings for him, but I'm still processing how hot he got over the summer, and my brain is struggling to remember why it would be a bad idea to lean over and kiss him right now.

I slap his arm. "No. That would be impossible. By the way, you're not allowed to leave me for a whole summer ever again."

"Well, that might be a problem, since I already got invited back for next summer."

"Seriously?!"

He nods. I can't help being proud of him, even if I am disappointed I'll have to go another summer without him around.

"Congrats. I know how big a deal that is—even if it means that you're abandoning me again." I smile at him so he knows I'm not really mad.

We pull into the parking lot, and I move my hand toward the handle when Jack stops me.

"Hang on." He reaches into the back, grabs his backpack, and then runs around to my side. He opens my door for me, and my jaw practically hits the floor. I was not expecting that. He's never done that for me before, and I'm sure my smile is a mile wide when I finally make eye contact with him. He just smiles back and then we walk together toward the main entrance.

This is going to be a good year. I can already tell.

TWO

Jack

When the hell did Paige get so gorgeous?

The thought keeps intruding every time I sneak a glance at my best friend sitting in the seat next to me while our history teacher, Mr. Morris, rambles on about who knows what—well, I'd probably know if I could concentrate for longer than ten seconds.

I can't stop replaying the moment when she opened the door this morning. For a second I was worried I might come in my pants because of how hot she got over the summer. Has she always been this beautiful? I mean, I knew that Paige was cute, but something definitely changed over the summer. Maybe it's because I was away for a couple of months and now I'm seeing her with fresh eyes. Whatever it is, it's got me all kinds of distracted and my body in a constant state of arousal that I've been fighting all day.

I sneak another glance. My gaze instantly lands on her plump pink lips that look shiny from her lip gloss, but it quickly drops to admire the way her dress hugs her in all the right places. I wiggle in my seat subtly, suddenly uncomfortable with the—once again—tightening of my pants. I've got to stop thinking about Paige this way, but damn, she looks so good.

Unlike me, she seems completely unaffected by my presence. She's focused on our teacher and taking notes dutifully like the good student she is. At least one of us can concentrate. I wonder if she'll let me copy her notes later. Maybe I can invite her over under the pretense of copying her notes but then make a move.

What the fuck am I thinking? This is Paige, for fuck's sake. She's my best friend. She's the one person in my life who has never cared about my parents' wealth or my popularity. Hell, she's the one who's always calling me out if I start to get too cocky. I can't fuck things up with her.

But, goddamn, I can't stop thinking about her either...and not in a purely friendly way. There is nothing wholesome about the thoughts swimming around nonstop in my head right now— even when she's less than three feet away from me.

I glance over at her again and catch her looking at me—or my arms more specifically. She turns away quickly, a blush creeping across her cheeks that makes her look even hotter if that's even possible at this point.

Did Paige just check me out? Is she feeling this too? Fuck, I hope so.

After what feels like forever, the class ends, and I walk out into the hall with Paige. She tucks a lock of hair behind her ear, suddenly shy with me. Paige hasn't been shy with me since we were five and I taught her how to swing, but I kind of like that I seem to make her a little nervous now. It's causing this adorable blush to stay on her cheeks, and I really like that. I put my hand on the small of her back and pull her into a secluded walkway. I quickly glance behind me to make sure no one is coming down this way before facing her.

"Jack? What's up?" She's looking at me like I'm being weird, which makes sense since I *am* acting weird, but I'm suddenly desperate to get her alone.

"I...I couldn't focus in Morris's class. Would you be down to come over to my house tonight so I can copy your notes?"

She quirks her brow, still confused, but also maybe amused. "Sure, or I could just give you my notebook now. You can give it back to me tomorrow."

"No," I say too quickly. If she gives it to me now, then I lose my excuse to hang out with her after practice. "It would be better if you just came over...you know, so I can...ask you to clarify your notes if I've got a question...or something."

"Okaayyy, sure. Did that really require you pulling me into this hallway? You're acting like you're about to do something illegal." She laughs at me nervously like she thinks I'm losing my mind.

To be fair, I might be. I'm trying to think of a valid excuse for my odd behavior, but she looks so beautiful looking at me with those big brown eyes that match her long, wavy hair, I can't stop myself.

Before I lose my nerve, I whisper, "No, but this did." Then, I lean down and kiss her.

Her lips are soft, just like I imagined they'd be. She makes a little moan and leans into me, kissing me back thoroughly and causing me to get hard again instantly—not like that's been a big challenge today. Her moan is, hands down, the sexiest sound I've ever heard. I kiss her deeper, holding her close to me and feeling her soft curves against my hard body, which only makes me wish we were truly alone and not still at school where anyone could walk up to us. Regardless, I'm going to take full advantage of this moment. My tongue snakes out to slide along the seam of her lips, and they open for me on a gasp.

I groan a little, kissing her harder, our tongues dancing with each other as if they were always made to do this. I've never wanted anyone this badly before, and it should probably weird me out that it's my best friend who's making me feel this way. But it doesn't. Everything about Paige pressed against me feels right.

The bell rings loudly, trilling along the hall and signaling that I'm likely going to be late for my next class. Paige pulls away, and I take great pleasure when I notice her eyes are dazed and slightly glassy and her perfect pink lips are plump and wet. She looks perfect. A smile breaks across her gorgeous face, and I can't help matching it with a big smile of my own.

"Pick me up after you get out of football practice. See you tonight." Paige gets on her tiptoes and kisses me briefly—too briefly—on the lips before she rushes to her next class.

I lean against the wall and take a deep breath, not caring in the slightest that I'm going to be late for class.

I just kissed Paige, and she kissed me back.

I've kissed a girl before—Jenny Blake at a football party my freshman year—but it was never like that. Even the brief kiss I gave Paige in seventh grade just to see what it was like doesn't compare to what just happened.

The problem is now all I can think about is how badly I want to kiss her again, which is going to make the rest of the day away from her absolute torture. I turn and walk down the hall toward my next class, not even bothering to hide the smile glued to my face.

THREE

Paige

Jack should be here any minute, and I'm sitting in my room like a nervous wreck, fidgeting with my backpack strap as I relive our kiss in the hallway in glorious technicolored detail. The way his lips caressed mine and then the brush of his tongue into my mouth. My skin prickles, my nerve endings lighting up across my arms simply thinking about how amazing that kiss was.

I've only ever really kissed one other boy before—Brody Kemper, who kissed like a fish. It was disgusting...and sloppy. I've always secretly wondered what it would be like to kiss Jack again, and now that I know, I don't ever want to stop. The kiss in the hallway today was nothing like our brief first kiss in seventh grade.

But that kiss also just completely changed the dynamic for our friendship. Does he even realize that? What did that kiss mean to him? Is it too much to hope that Jack wants me to be his girlfriend? He hasn't had any serious girlfriends in the past— thank God, since I'm positive now that I wouldn't be able to hide my jealousy—but I know he's kissed other girls before, or at least one other girl. He told me about Jenny Blake after that football party freshman year. I was relieved when he confessed that he thought it was bad, and I remember laughing my ass off when he told me how scared he was that she was going to suck his face off. It was also that moment that gave me my first clue that my feelings for Jack had officially strayed from the friend zone, or else I wouldn't have been as bothered as I was that he kissed her at all.

Truthfully, I've always thought Jack and I would end up together. It almost feels too good to be true now that it looks like we're actually heading that way. But I still have some lingering doubts. Jack's been so focused on football and never seemed interested in wanting anything serious with anyone. What if he doesn't see this as a long-term thing, but more of a friends with benefits arrangement, like some of the guys on his football team? I'd be devastated.

The doorbell rings, and I immediately jump up from my bed and rush downstairs. My dad beats me to the door and greets Jack with his usual warm smile. My dad loves Jack and would probably be thrilled if we got together, especially since Jack is like the athletic son my dad never had. Both of my older brothers are insanely nerdy—Trevor is in robotics and wants to be a mechanical engineer when he gets older, and Connor is a hardcore gamer.

Jack gives my dad a handshake and a smile before he catches sight of me. His blue eyes brighten, and his smile grows as his gaze lingers slightly longer on my lips. My cheeks heat with a blush that causes me to silently curse my fair skin while my lips tilt up in a smile that matches Jack's. I swear all my feelings are on display, but Jack doesn't seem to mind. His smile stays glued to his face.

I turn to give my dad a hug goodbye and notice his gaze darting between the two of us and a slight furrow of his brow. If he notices that something's changed between us, he doesn't say anything. Instead, he leans in and hugs me tightly before turning to Jack.

"Take care of my baby girl and have her back before her ten o'clock curfew."

"Yes, sir."

We're both silent as we walk to Jack's car and as he opens the passenger door for me again. When he gets into the car, he turns to me and says quietly, "You look beautiful, Paige."

My blush deepens, but I can't help smiling at him—have I even stopped smiling since he got to my house? "You too."

Wait. What?

Oh my God. I close my eyes as my cheeks flame for a completely different reason than before. "Um, actually...you know...I meant handsome. You look handsome. Not beautiful. Guys aren't beautiful. That would be weird." Crap. I'm rambling. I've never been nervous with Jack before, especially not like this, and now I sound like a complete moron.

Fantastic, Paige. Nice one.

He laughs and leans over the middle console, and the second his lips meet mine all my panic disappears. It's like the entire world stops spinning while his lips are pressed gently against mine. Having him this close to me is dangerous. God, he smells so good.

He pulls back and looks at me, his eyes holding an unfamiliar tenderness. "I like you all nervous like this—it's new."

I smack his arm, causing him to laugh more before he pulls out onto the road taking us to his house. The ride is comfortable, which isn't surprising because Jack has always made me feel incredibly comfortable with him. We can talk about anything without it getting weird. It's one of the reasons he's my best friend. He's always been my protector and confidant, and I don't ever want that to change. I can't imagine not having him in my life which is why all these new, intense feelings kind of terrify me. I want him more than I've ever wanted anyone, but I don't want to risk losing him for good. I couldn't handle that.

When we get to his house, we head straight up to his room where we regularly study, but it was always innocent before. Right now, heading up to his room, it doesn't feel innocent at all. The air seems to sizzle from the tension swirling around us, and studying is the last thing on my mind. Based on the heated look Jack gives me, I'm pretty sure it's the last thing on his mind too.

"Where are your parents tonight?" I ask.

"They're at an art gala in support of a show curated by Senator Rothburg's daughter."

Jack's dad is a reasonably famous lawyer representing several Congress members from Washington, Oregon, and California, as well as numerous celebrities. They're constantly away at one event or another, but I've always been impressed by their devotion to their only child. They've never once missed one of Jack's football games. I know it means a lot to him since he wants to make his parents proud. Honestly, how could they not be proud of him?

Jack mostly closes the door to his room. He leaves it open a smidge, I'm assuming so he can hear the door downstairs open when his parents get home. But the act itself has my heart galloping erratically in my chest; he's never closed the door like this before during one of our previous study sessions.

He moves slowly toward me, his eyes darker than I've ever seen them, and takes my backpack off my shoulder, gently placing it on the ground. He stands in front of me and reaches with one hand to tuck a lock of my hair behind my ear. I look down, smirking bashfully toward the floor in some weak attempt at hiding my feelings from him, but I know it's useless. There's no way he hasn't clued in to all that I'm feeling.

Jack pushes my chin up gently with his index finger so that

I'm looking at him. "Paige, I think we need to talk." His tone is serious, his gaze no longer heated but cautious and reserved.

My heart plummets as doubt suffuses me. Those aren't exactly the best words to hear. They're almost always followed by something terrible.

"Okay," I whisper.

"You know you're my best friend, right?"

I nod, and he continues. "We've always told each other everything, right?"

I nod again. I have no idea where he's going with this, but I can't speak. My heart is in my throat right now, preparing for the worst. He's going to let me down easy, and I'm going to have to pretend to not be completely and utterly shattered that I have unrequited feelings for my best friend.

"I have to tell you something." He looks deep into my eyes like he's searching for something from me. Then he whispers, "I have a crush on someone."

Oh, God. My chest feels like it's caving in as my heart breaks and my worst fears are realized. I knew today was too good to be true. That kiss in the hallway meant nothing. And what the hell was that kiss in the car? Was that some pity kiss because he knew he was about to let me down easy? Ugh, I feel so incredibly stupid right now. The burn of tears stings the back of my eyes, but I refuse to cry in front of Jack. Not now.

He continues on, his words coming out a little faster. "I probably shouldn't be feeling this way about her, but I can't seem to stop myself. She's absolutely gorgeous, and I can't stop thinking about her."

I can't breathe. It's like every word out of his mouth is designed to suck the air from my lungs and make my stomach tighten in knots from the invisible blow. My poor heart aches in my chest as I attempt to remind myself that this was always a possibility. I knew there was a chance things would go this way, but I wasn't as prepared as I should've been. Lesson learned.

I can't stay here any longer. I glance toward the door before reluctantly looking back at Jack. I hate how handsome he is and how badly I still want him, even as he talks about liking someone else. His mouth turns down and his eyes get a slightly panicked look as his chest starts to rise and fall faster. If I wasn't fighting against my own heartbreak right now, I'd ask him if he was okay.

"Paige?"

I can't be this close to him anymore. Pushing him away, I avoid his questioning gaze and try to think of an exit strategy.

"You know what, I just remembered that I, um..." Shit, I can feel the tears as they start to stream down my face, and I suck in a deep breath before looking down. "I have to go. I hope it works out with your crush." My voice cracks at the end, and I wince, hoping he didn't hear it.

I reach for my backpack lying on the floor by his feet, but he stops me.

"Damn. I messed this up. Paige, my crush is..." He's observing me carefully, and all I can do is wish the ground would swallow me up right now. I still can't believe how badly I misinterpreted this whole situation.

"Paige, you're my crush. I have a crush on you."

It takes a minute for the words to fully register, but as soon as they do, my gaze shoots to his. The tears slow as my brain finally catches up with the words that came out of his mouth.

Jack brushes the tears from my face. "Paige, did you hear me?" His normally bright and happy eyes are filled with worry, and his jaw moves like he's nibbling the inside of his lip.

"Please say something," he says, his voice hoarse and nervous.

"You like me? Like, like me like me?" God, I sound so much like a teenage girl right now, I want to vomit.

A small smile graces his gorgeous face. "Yeah, I like you. A lot, actually. I don't want to mess up our friendship, but I also don't want to miss out on seeing where this could go."

He gently clasps my hand in his, brushing the top of it with his thumb. A shiver goes through my body, and goosebumps break out across my skin at the contact. My heart has started to slow to a more normal beat, and my emotions are calming down as his words wrap around me.

Jack likes me.

"So, you want to date me?"

He cups the back of his neck with his hand, rubbing it a little self-consciously. "Well, yeah. Do you want to date me?"

"Yes," I whisper. I can't believe this is happening. Pinch me. I must be dreaming.

His face breaks out in the radiant smile I'm so used to seeing on him. "So, you'll be my girlfriend?"

I can't help but smile back at him, especially hearing the excitement in his voice. "Yes."

I giggle and throw my arms around his neck, kissing him like I've wanted to since he picked me up. His arms go around my waist, and he holds me close to him as our lips and tongues explore each other's mouths.

This is really happening.

I'm finally getting everything I've ever dreamed.

FOUR

Jack

Despite not being able to think about anything but Paige for the past month, I've still managed to do well in my classes and on the football field. I'm not your average dumb jock—something I pride myself on. I get As and Bs and maintain a solid GPA while being the starting quarterback for our school's undefeated football team.

As much as I love football, none of that compares to the thrill I get every time I enter school holding Paige's hand. I look over at her walking down the hall next to me, her petite hand in my much larger one. She's wearing my letterman jacket, her hair falling softly halfway down her back. She's honestly never looked sexier.

I overheard one of the senior players talking in the locker room about how his girlfriend surprised him by wearing only his letterman jacket and nothing else. He said it was the best sex he'd ever had. Looking at Paige, I keep thinking about what she would look like wearing only my letterman jacket.

Fuck, that's not a smart thought to have when walking down the halls. The last thing I need is to pop another boner at school

—something that has become a constant problem since Paige and I started dating.

I'm a teenage boy. I was thinking about sex pretty regularly before I even had a girlfriend. Now that I do, and that girlfriend is Paige—who is smoking hot—I honestly can't stop thinking about what sex will be like with her. But neither of us are ready to take that step. We've talked about it. We're both virgins, and right now I'm kind of thankful for that. I love the idea that I'll be the first guy Paige is with. The thought of anyone else touching her makes my blood boil.

It's moments like this when I realize that I can't imagine my life without Paige in it. I know I'm only sixteen and way too young to think about marriage and all that, but I know Paige is the one. I've loved her as a friend for most of my life and now... well, I haven't told her yet, but I'm in love with her.

She glances at me, her gorgeous brown eyes filled with happiness, and I swear my heart stops. Goddamn, she's so fucking gorgeous.

"What are you smiling about?" she asks, her lilting voice making my pants feel tighter while the rest of my body feels like it's floating. I didn't even realize I was smiling, but I shouldn't be surprised. I don't think I've stopped smiling in the last month.

"Just thinking about our date this weekend." I squeeze her hand, and she smiles at me.

How did I get so lucky? Some days I really want to go back to five-year-old me and give that kid a big fucking high five for befriending this girl.

I pick Paige up at seven o'clock. It's a Saturday night, so her curfew is midnight instead of her weekday curfew of ten o'clock.

Her dad seems happy that we're dating, although her mom seems a little cautious. I think she's worried about what happens if we break up, but that's never going to happen. I'm in too deep already. Paige makes me feel things I never knew were possible. She pushes me to be my best, supports me, and makes me feel like the happiest guy in the world. Why would I ever give that up?

Paige comes down the stairs, and my gaze scans up her body, my breath stopping in my chest. It can't be healthy that my heart keeps stopping like this, right? I don't think it's normal. None of the other guys talk about feeling like this with their girls.

Reminding myself to breathe, I reach out to hold Paige's hand. She's wearing a blue dress with a lace print design that hugs her upper body and then flares out at the waist. It stops about midthigh, showing off enough leg for me to be sufficiently horny at the sight of her. But, let's be real, I'm a guy—I'd be horny looking at her ankles.

I give her a simple kiss on the cheek, instead of kissing her enticing luscious pink lips like I really want to since both her parents are standing right there. Putting my hand on the small of her back, I lead her toward my car after saying our goodbyes to her parents.

Her hand rests casually in mine, our fingers laced together and resting on her thigh as I drive to the seafood restaurant that's gotten great reviews. Paige likes simple things, but I really want to spoil her and make her as happy as she makes me, so I thought I'd treat her to a fancy date instead of our usual burger joint down the street from my house.

When we get to the restaurant, our conversation flows, like always. She asks all about my away game last night, and I tell her how close it was. We were playing West Hills High School. They have one of the best teams in the league and put up one hell of a fight. We won, but just barely. It wasn't my best night.

Paige comes to every home game but can't usually go to the away games. Her parents don't let her ride in a car with anyone but me, and since I have to ride the bus for away games, she doesn't typically come. I'm hoping next season they'll loosen up and let her ride with one of the other players' girlfriends because I want her at all my games. Her smile has this odd ability to help relax me when I'm playing. It sets me on fire the rest of the time, but it's calming when I can glance up at the stands and see her smiling down at me. I definitely could've used it last night.

After dinner, we walk along the water. The weather has cooled down significantly in the past week, and the sun is just starting to set. There's a chill in the air, but the view is unbeatable. The beauty of the orange, yellow, and pink colors of the sky meeting the deep blue of the water is breathtaking.

When she shivers, I take off my jacket and drape it over her shoulders while we sit at a wooden bench at the end of a pier, and I put my arm around her. I could hold Paige forever and never get tired of it. I thought holding a football was the best feeling in the world until Paige and I started dating.

She sighs and leans against me. "Tonight has been perfect." She turns to me, the tenderness in her eyes making my heart beat a little faster. "Actually, every night with you is perfect."

This is the moment I've been waiting for. She's looking at me with that beautiful smile on her lips and her chocolate-brown eyes sparkling.

I tuck a lock of hair behind her ear. "I love you, Paige."

Her eyes widen slightly before her smile grows, and she whispers, "I love you, too, Jack."

She leans forward, pressing her soft lips to mine, and I kiss her deeply before pulling back and giving her my classic smirk.

"Just so we're clear, I mean that I'm in love with you, as in I love you more than a friend."

She slaps my arm—I not so secretly love when she does that—and laughs. I've never heard a better sound in all my life, and it's my new mission in life to make sure I always make her laugh. Unable to hold back, I lean in to kiss her again.

Her tongue darts between my lips, and the kiss goes from soft to frantic in a heartbeat. I grab the back of her head and devour her mouth, our tongues dancing together. We've gotten really good at making out—I mean *really* good. I feel one of her hands slide from my knee up toward my crotch, and my brain nearly short-circuits. She's not doing what I think she's doing, is she?

She is.

Her hand glides across the stiffening bulge in my pants, and the heat from her touch feels scalding even with the layers of clothing separating her skin from mine. Despite having dated for a month, we haven't done anything but make out. This is the first time she's touched me like this, and even over my pants, it feels fucking incredible. Her other hand is in my hair, our lips still frantically molding together, tongues gliding across each other. My breathing hitches as she continues to caress me, and I let out a tortured groan.

Oh fuck, this feels good. Too good. I'm going to totally jizz in my pants if she doesn't stop. I pull away from her, panting for breath, and quickly move her hand off me. Paige looks dazed—and sexy as hell with that damn blush on her face and her lips red and wet from our kissing—when her eyes finally open and meet mine.

"Why did you stop? Did I do something wrong?" She looks a little unsure, and I absolutely cannot stand the idea of her thinking anything negative right now.

"You definitely were doing it right. It felt so good, Paige," I say, dropping a too brief kiss to her lips. "Too good, if you know what I mean." It takes her a second before her blush deepens.

"Oh." She giggles, and she looks so fucking sexy that I can't help myself. I reach back over and kiss her again before reluctantly pulling away.

"I should probably take you home."

"It's still early. We could go for a drive."

I'm only slightly more experienced than Paige, but we both know what "going for a drive" means around here. It means going to wherever the hot spot is and hooking up. The definition of hooking up tends to vary. Several guys on the football team have used it to describe full-on sex, while a few others use it to mean that they did everything but sex. Either way, it means more than kissing.

But I have no intention of taking Paige's virginity in my car's back seat, no matter how nice of a car it is. I want our first time together to be special and unforgettable. Paige is a hopeless romantic; I want to give her the fairytale she's always dreamed of.

All that being said, I've jacked off multiple times a day thinking about Paige. I can't help but want to go a little further than just making out, especially after a month of tasting her perfect lips.

"Okay. Let's go for a drive."

The Sharks are playing dirty tonight. I've lost count of how many times I've been sacked during this damn game. I can see Paige in the bleachers, her cheeks rosy from the cold, her fingers fidgeting nervously in front of her. She's confessed more than once how worried she gets when I get sacked. I can only imagine what tonight is doing to her since I've taken more hard hits tonight than this whole season combined.

I take a deep breath and turn my attention to focus on the

huddle. We're down by six. We haven't lost a homecoming game in ten seasons, and we're not going to lose now that I'm starting quarterback. I call the play, and we get in position. I focus on the field, the players around me, and block out the sounds of the crowd.

This place is sacred to me. I love the adrenaline rush I get when I'm on the field—the high from the pressure and the nervous energy that comes with trying to complete a play before I get tackled by the opposing side. The excitement that shoots through my body when I lead my team to victory is incredible.

The only thing that's ever felt better than this is being with Paige.

I can hear the opposing team muttering insults and swearing, typical behavior on the field. I hear #87 on the opposing team mumble some stupid "yo momma" insult, and the tension between the teams is almost palpable. The Eastside Sharks are our biggest rivals, and this year their talent is better than ever.

My mind zeros in on the play—everything disappearing around me except for the players on the field and the football that's ready and waiting. O'Connor snaps the ball to me, and I look around for my receivers. I can see a Sharks player come barreling toward me, but none of my guys are open. I don't want to lose yardage, and I'm really sick of getting sacked every other minute. In a last-ditch effort to end the play without setting us back, I chuck the ball wide toward nothing. It's a dangerous move. The ref could call intentional grounding, but it's all I can think of in that moment. Luckily, the ref doesn't call it. My coach, on the other hand, looks pissed at me. It was a dick move, and we both know it. I shake it off and focus on the game.

We get back in line, and O'Connor snaps the ball to me. This time, Ashby is open. The ball spirals beautifully through the air and lands smoothly in his extended hands. Ashby runs toward the end zone and makes it right as another player tackles him.

Touchdown!

Walters, our kicker, boots the ball straight through the goalposts, and victory is ours.

I look up to the stands and spot Paige jumping up and down, cheering, her smile radiant and her eyes filled with joy. I swear she's my biggest fan and supporter. That girl is unbelievable, and she's all mine. On instinct, I run over and jump up into the stands, pulling her to me in a deep kiss.

"Fuller!" my coach shouts behind me.

Paige breaks from the kiss breathless, and I turn back to my coach.

"Sorry, Coach. Had to kiss my girl. She's my good luck charm."

I smile at Paige, give her one more peck, and then head back to the field. We shake hands with the other team and then head to the locker room. The guys are buzzing with excitement—nothing beats the thrill of a victory. And I'm right there with them, flying high on the energy going around the room. It was a close game, but sometimes those are the best because they keep us focused. We have to work for our win, which makes it more meaningful in the end.

Paige is waiting for me when I walk out of the locker room, showered and changed. She runs into my arms, and I spin her around. Sometimes I still can't quite believe that this girl is all mine; it feels a little too good to be true.

She smiles up at me. "I was on the edge of my seat that whole game, but I'm so proud of you! You were amazing out there."

Her belief in me is one of the reasons I love her so much—that and because she's beautiful inside and out. Paige is, without a doubt, one of the most caring girls I've ever met. I'm a lucky guy.

"Hey, wanna go to a celebratory party at the lake? The guys invited us out."

"Sure. I just need to text my parents to let them know."

After Paige gets the all clear from her parents, we head to the lake. It's an absolute madhouse by the time we get there. I don't know how they get away with doing this every year without the cops coming. Maybe because it's secluded enough from town, but still, it's insanity. There are cars everywhere with their headlights on to light up the party. There are a ton of high school kids milling around and a bonfire down near the water.

I grab Paige's hand to keep her close to me as we wander through the people. Music is playing loudly from someone's car, and I see a bunch of my teammates dancing with their girl-friends, or whatever girl they happen to be dating this week.

My teammate and friend Nate O'Connor and his girlfriend, Kayla, make their way over to us, and we end up chatting around the bonfire for over an hour. By eleven, we've all had some of the alcohol O'Connor snuck out with him, and I'm definitely feeling it. I can't stop touching Paige. I can tell she's feeling the effects of the alcohol too, because she keeps giggling and touching me back.

I desperately want to get her alone and reenact that night in my car from last week when we went for a drive and she let me finger her. God, she was so hot—well, she's always hot, but watching her come apart like that was something out of this world. And the feel of her hands on me when she returned the favor is permanently burned into my memory.

Once O'Connor and Kayla start making out, it's pretty easy to pull Paige away and take her closer to the trees where we can have a little privacy. I need to get my hands on her bare skin.

We make it to the tree line, and I push her back gently against one of the tall trees. She's laughing softly, her eyes bright from the buzz of alcohol, even though she only had one drink. If she'd had any more, I wouldn't even consider doing this, but we're both only slightly buzzed.

I kiss her deeply, my hand sliding up her shirt to cup her breast. She moans in my mouth, and I lose all sense of control. I kiss her neck, sucking on it hard, and move down. Her shirt is in my way, so I quickly pull it off and slide her bra down. She inhales sharply as I suck on her nipple. I love watching her facial expressions when we're like this. It's a better high than being on the field.

Her back arches, pushing her breast farther into my mouth, and I can't get enough of her. I'm about to unbutton her pants when we hear laughing getting closer. Paige inhales sharply, and I quickly cover her with my body. No way in hell am I letting someone else see Paige like this. All my protective instincts are on high alert. The voices come closer and round the corner to where I thought we were pretty well hidden.

"Fuller, that you?" It's Donahue, one of our senior defensive linemen. "It is you!"

He slurs his words, and I can just barely make out from the light of the moon that he is completely wasted. The girl on his arm looks pretty trashed too. Before I can respond to Donahue, the girl says something to him and then immediately turns and vomits on the ground.

I think it's safe to say the mood is officially dead. I can't hook up with Paige after watching a random girl vomit all her beer, which just so happens to trigger Donahue.

He exclaims, "Oh, fuck, that's so gross," before he chokes on the last word and projectile vomit comes out of his mouth.

Let me tell you, there's nothing more sobering—or disgusting—than watching two people vomit next to each other.

I keep Paige covered while she puts her bra and shirt back on. I check on Donahue and his date to ensure they'll be okay before heading back toward the party. I fill O'Connor in on Donahue, and he proceeds to grab a couple of bottles of water and head over to find him. With Paige's hand firmly back in mine, we make a hasty retreat.

"Well, this night didn't turn out quite like I expected."

She laughs softly. "That's okay. We always have tomorrow."

Ah, yes. The homecoming dance. I definitely plan to get my hands on Paige again tomorrow.

FIVE

Paige

"How do I look?"

My mom and dad look up, and both instantly break into huge grins. I think my dad might even be tearing up a little.

"Dad," I chide, "don't cry. This isn't even prom. It's just homecoming."

"Paige, allow me to be a dad. And right now, I'm a dad who can't believe how grown up his little girl has gotten. You look beautiful, honey."

I blush a little—I'm a daddy's girl through and through. "Thanks, Daddy."

"When will Jack be here?" my mom asks while pulling out her camera.

As if on cue, the doorbell rings, and Jack is standing on the other side in a navy blue suit. Jesus, he cleans up well. I mean, I love him in a pair of jeans and a T-shirt with his letterman jacket over it, but this cleaned up look is...yummy. His eyes light up, and he inhales sharply when he sees me in my form-fitting, short, navy blue dress with just a hint of cleavage.

"Paige, you look gorgeous."

I smile brightly at him. "Thank you. You don't look so bad yourself."

"You ready to go?"

"Not quite yet, you two." My mom stops us. "I want some pictures."

The thumping of pop music blares from the speakers set up at the DJ booth when we enter the school gym, where the homecoming dance is being held. It's decorated with glow in the dark stars and big, round Styrofoam balls that have been painted to look like planets. It's a galaxy theme to go with the tagline "Out of This World." It's totally cheesy, but the room looks stunning. They've got string lights set up, so it's romantic, but also faintly looks like they could be stars in the sky.

Jack and I dance and laugh through more than a dozen songs before I decide I've experienced enough of homecoming. We posed for pictures, danced, hung out with friends. Now, I just want to get him alone and finish what we started last night.

We go to our favorite spot—a park with a lot of big, beautiful trees that offer privacy and rarely has anyone around this late at night. The second Jack puts the car in park, we start frantically pawing at each other. I'm relieved to see that I'm not the only one feeling like this. Jack can't seem to get enough of me, and frankly, I can't get enough of him either.

I can't help but wonder if this is normal, to want someone this desperately and passionately even though we're only sixteen.

I'm distracted from my thoughts as Jack's mouth crashes against mine. His lips press hard against my own as his tongue darts out to glide along the seam of my lips, before sliding inside. Our tongues continue the dance they've perfected while his hands roam over my body. I feverishly try to undo the buttons of his shirt, desperate to feel my skin on his. My whole body is vibrating with need, and it almost feels like I'm on fire. I didn't know it was possible to want someone this badly.

He breaks from my lips, his mouth kissing and sucking down my neck to my collarbone, while his fingers urgently wrap around my back to pull my zipper down. With his shirt undone, I roam my hands up and down the flat, toned planes of his stomach. He lets out a shuddering breath—I love how my touch affects him.

"Fuck, Paige. What are you doing to me?" His lips barely leave my skin as he speaks, his fingers gently tugging down the top of my dress. "I never want to stop touching you."

I whisper seductively in his ear, "Then don't."

I don't know where this wanton version of me comes from, but I'm kind of loving it. Jack makes me feel incredibly confident and sexy. I'm never embarrassed to be forward with him or tell him what I want. I've overheard other girls talking about faking it with their boyfriends or just doing what their boyfriends want to do, and I can't imagine why they would stay with those guys. It's never once been like that with Jack.

I slide my hands down his abs, following his happy trail, and begin unbuckling his pants. Slipping my hand underneath his boxers, I wrap my fingers around his hard as steel, yet velvety soft erection causing him to groan loudly before whispering my name with a tone of astonished reverence. It doesn't take long for Jack to fall apart, and it's a heady feeling knowing that I can bring him to his knees like this.

He turns to me, his eyes half-lidded with lust and satisfaction. "Your turn."

One thing I love most about my intimacy with Jack is that the pleasure isn't one-sided. Apparently, that's rare for a high school relationship like ours.

Jack slips my panties down my legs and slides his hands up. The pleasure I feel when I'm with him is unreal. I never knew I could feel like this. There literally aren't enough words to describe how amazing it is, but the problem is I never want it to stop. I feel like I'm getting addicted to Jack and the incredible feelings he evokes. Suddenly, he rotates his fingers inside me and starts hitting a spot that triggers blinding pleasure. I explode around him and collapse back against the seat, completely blissed out.

When I finally open my eyes, Jack is smiling at me. "I love watching you come. It's the hottest thing I've ever seen."

I give him a sated smile. "You're more than welcome to make me come as much as you want."

He leans across the console to kiss me deeply. "I love you, Paige."

"I love you too," I sigh, content in this moment with the boy I love more than anything.

He pulls back, giving me his gorgeous lopsided grin before he sits back in his seat and starts buttoning his pants.

"What are you doing?"

"Buckling my pants. What's it look like I'm doing?"

I put my hand on his belt to stop him. "What if I want more?"

"More?"

"Yeah. I've been thinking about it a lot. I think...I think I'm ready for us to go all the way."

"Paige..." His voice is pained, and all my confidence immediately evaporates.

"You don't want to?"

I can tell he hears the insecurity in my tone because he immediately cups my face in his hands and leans his forehead against mine. "Paige, I want nothing more than to go all the way with you. But I'm not going to take your virginity in the backseat of my car. You deserve way more than that. I also don't want to do it until you are for sure ready. I won't push you into this. But please don't ever doubt how badly I want to be with you like that, because I do. Desperately. I promise when the time is right, and we're both sure, we'll lose our virginity together, okay?"

I nod my head and whisper, "Okay."

I love Jack more than anything—there's no doubt in my mind about that—but he's probably right; it's too soon. We've only been together for two months. Having sex is a big deal, and I really don't want to lose my virginity in the backseat of his car. I always imagined it would be somewhere romantic and special.

Once again, I'm thankful that Jack is the one I'm experiencing all this with. He doesn't pressure me, and he knows me well enough to know what I really want and need. We can wait. He's still going to be my first—and hopefully my only. We have plenty of time before we take that next step.

SIX

Jack

It's been six months—six fucking perfect months with Paige. I love her more every day. The guys on my football team tease me all the time for being pussy whipped, but I don't even try to deny it. Hell yes, I'm pussy whipped by Paige. The guys don't get it because they don't love their girls like I love mine. I can see my whole future with Paige, now more than ever.

We still haven't had sex yet. Since that first night four months ago, we've done everything except for sex. Paige has been saying she's ready—for sure ready—but I didn't want to push her. I know it's a big deal for girls. It's a big deal for me, too, but I care a lot less about the specifics of how it happens. But I know Paige always imagined something special and romantic. I've been trying to plan it out. I was thinking about waiting until prom, but that's still two months away, and it seems a little cliché. I'll figure it out. I've got plenty of time.

I pull up to Paige's house and see her already sitting on the porch steps. I get out of the car and head over to her. It's not until I get closer that I notice tears are sliding down her face, and her eyes are blotchy and puffy like she's been crying for a while. I run the rest of the distance to her and sit down, wrapping her in my arms.

"Paige? What's wrong?"

She hiccups and bursts into more tears, burying her face in my chest as her body heaves from her sobs. I have no idea how to handle this. I've seen Paige cry before, but never like this.

"Paige. I need you to talk to me, baby. What happened?"

She lifts her head, and a look of anguish crosses her face. "We're moving to Chicago."

I feel like I've just been tackled on the field, hard. I can't breathe, and my heart feels like someone is squeezing it while simultaneously trying to rip it from my chest. I can barely manage the words, "What? When?"

She sniffles, and tears continue to pour down her face. "Next month. My dad's company is transferring him. It's a promotion apparently." Her voice drops as tears continue to stream from her eyes, the anguish on her face telling me this doesn't feel like a promotion, but a death sentence.

This can't be happening. She can't leave. Not now, not when we're so perfect together. My brain is struggling to process this information. Apart from last summer, when I was away at football camp, Paige and I have never really been separated. I can't imagine her not being at school or coming to my games or just being around. My whole life seems so profoundly entwined with hers.

She starts sobbing again, and I hold her close to me. I don't know how to fix this. I don't know how to take away her pain when I'm struggling with my own. I thought Paige and I had forever.

We're only sixteen. Can we really make a long-distance relationship work?

She hugs me tightly and whispers, "I don't want to leave you, Jack. I love you so much. I don't want to go."

I kiss her hair and hold her tighter against me. "I know, baby. I don't want you to go either."

I'm struggling to keep my own emotions in check right now, but I need to stay strong for Paige. We have to make this work. I can't live without her.

SEVEN

Paige

Jack stayed for dinner but left shortly after. We didn't talk much after I dropped the whole "I'm moving" bomb.

I hate this. I can't leave Jack. He's been around nearly my entire life. I can't stand the idea of not seeing him every day. This last summer was practically torture, and that was with the knowledge that he'd be home before school started. Not to mention the fact that we weren't even a couple at that point. Everything is different now, and this time, there's no guarantee of when we'll see each other again. Neither of us has a job, and it's not exactly cheap to fly across the country to visit your significant other, especially when you're a teenager.

My dad is so excited about this promotion, which makes all of this significantly harder. I want to be happy for him, but I can't. I can't get past the fact that he's ruining everything.

I'm sitting curled up on my bed, silently crying, when my mom softly knocks on the door before coming in. I glance at her before turning back to the window. I can't stop the tears that are streaming down my face, so I don't even try as she comes to sit at the end of the bed and places her hand on my ankle.

"Oh, honey. I'm so sorry. I know this is hard on you. Do you want to talk about it?"

"What's there to talk about? I don't get a say in this move, do I?"

I sound like a sullen teen, and I hate that. I've always had an excellent relationship with my parents, but I can't help the slight anger present in my voice.

She looks down at her lap. "No, I guess you don't really get a say. It's going to be hard, but you know you can always keep in touch with Jack over the phone, and we could probably afford for you to come back to see him this summer."

"He's at football camp all summer."

"Oh. Right. Well, I'm sure we could work something out between his parents and figure out ways for you two to stay close. I know how much you mean to each other. I know I was a little...reserved when you two first got together, but I can see how that boy looks at you—it reminds me of how your dad looks at me. It's like the whole world revolves around you." She smiles.

"I love him so much, Mom," I whisper, my voice cracking at the end as the anguish in my heart seeps into my words. I'm going to miss him so much.

"I know, honey. If it's real love, then it'll work itself out in the end. Just because we move doesn't mean you and Jack can't be together."

"You really think we can make it work?"

"I think you can certainly try. If you two love each other, and I believe you do, I think you'll find a way to be together."

I can't help but hope that she's right. I want nothing more than to be with Jack. I want to be with him forever.

EIGHT

Jack

When I get home, my dad is sitting on the couch, watching a basketball game, but he mutes it as soon as he sees me.

"Jack? You okay?" he asks, his brows furrowed with concern and his mouth turned down in a frown.

"No."

I don't say anything else as I sit down next to him. I can feel the weight of his stare as he waits for me to elaborate, but I can't find the words. Instead, I stare unseeingly at the TV. I feel like my whole world is crashing down around me, and I'm trying to sort through everything that I'm feeling, but the only thing I can process is how much the thought of Paige leaving makes me feel dead inside.

"Jack." My dad speaks softly and puts his hand on my shoulder. "What's wrong? You've got me kind of worried over here, and I've got a whole slew of scenarios running through my head right now."

"Paige and her family are moving to Chicago." I don't even recognize the vacant voice as mine as the words leave my mouth like they're being ripped from my soul.

My dad lets out a deep exhale, and I think I hear him

murmur, "Thank God." I glare at him, immediately ready to defend Paige, although my dad's never been against us before.

"Sorry, I thought you were about to tell me you got Paige pregnant. I'm too young to be a grandpa."

"Dad!" He should know me better than that.

"Sorry. Okay, so Paige is moving. When?"

"Next month, I guess. Her dad got a promotion at work."

My voice breaks at the end, and I can't keep my emotions in check any longer. I feel my throat tightening and a burning behind my eyes. I'm trying so hard to hold it together. I haven't cried since I was a kid. But the idea of losing Paige has me gutted in a way I've never felt before.

My dad wraps his arm around me. "Oh, Jack. I'm sorry. I know how much she means to you."

"I love her," I whisper. "I love her so much. I can't imagine her not being here. Not being at my games or in my classes. She's been my best friend forever, and now she's so much more. She's everything."

Choking on the last word, I lose my fight with my emotions and cover my face with my hands. My dad sits there with his arms wrapped around me while I let everything out, and I'm grateful he doesn't try to fill the silence with meaningless words that won't fix the pain in my heart.

I don't know how long my dad and I sit there. When I finally manage to pull myself together, I see my mom standing in the doorway between the kitchen and the living room. Her lips are turned down in a frown, and there's no mistaking the worry in her eyes as she glances between my dad and me. My dad shakes his head at her like he's silently telling her he'll explain later. Good. I don't want to have to talk about this again. I don't know if I even can.

"I'm going to bed," I murmur as I stand up and start heading upstairs.

My dad calls out to me before I've even reached the third step. "It'll all work out, Jack. I know it doesn't feel like it right now, but it'll work out in the end. We'll figure it out, okay?"

I nod my head without looking at him and then continue up the stairs, my steps falling heavy on each stair and my mind burdened with what the future holds for us. I don't know how it'll work out. Chicago is 2,123 miles away. I looked it up when Paige went to the bathroom before dinner.

I want to believe my dad. I want what he said to be true more than anything else in the world, but I can't help the doubts that are slithering their way into my head.

Can we really make long distance work?

NINE

Paige

The sight of Jack standing on my front porch with flowers in his hand calms my frayed nerves and anxiety from last night. He's wearing jeans, a button-down shirt, and his letterman jacket. Damn, he looks good in that jacket. He smiles at me, but I can see the sadness in his eyes, the hollow, lost look that permeates his normally bright blue eyes. I could hardly sleep last night after telling him about the move, and when exhaustion did finally pull me under, it was a fitful night's sleep.

I smile faintly back at him. "Hey."

"Wanna go somewhere?"

I'd go anywhere with him. "Where'd you have in mind?"

"It's a surprise."

I smile a little brighter now. Jack is usually terrible about keeping secrets from me, so it must be something he thought of today. At some point, I know we need to talk about what things will be like when I leave, but I don't have the courage to bring it up. I don't want to hear him say that all this will end when I move.

"Okay. Let me grab my jacket."

We drive for nearly twenty minutes when I start to see familiar landmarks and can guess where we're going.

"Are we going to Chinook Point?"

He gives me a disgruntled look, which only makes me laugh because it's so obvious I've ruined the surprise. "Maybe...Okay, fine. Yes," he says.

He looks over at me, his eyes bright and heated and his lips quirked up in that boyish grin of his that I love so much. "We're going to the place where we had our first kiss."

"The lighthouse?" I ask softly.

"Mhmm."

We went on a field trip in seventh grade to the old, but still well-kept lighthouse at Chinook Point. I tripped on a log and Jack caught me. But after he caught me, he continued to hold my hand. He kept looking at our hands for a few minutes before he suddenly looked up at me, leaned in, and kissed me briefly on the lips. It was one of the first times I wondered if we might end up together, if maybe someday we'd be a real couple. But neither of us ever said anything after that kiss, so I assumed it wasn't a big deal to him. I honestly thought he'd forgotten all about it.

After we park, Jack pulls out a picnic basket and several blankets. He entwines the fingers of his free hand with mine and smiles down on me, his face so open and full of love it makes my heart beat faster in my chest. All signs of sadness from earlier are wiped from his eyes, and his happiness helps ease much of my own sadness.

We walk down the empty beach laughing and talking about nothing important until we reach the lighthouse, and he sets up the picnic in a secluded spot. I'm so impressed to see all the little details that he thought of. He made me my favorite sandwich—ham and Swiss on a French roll—and even brought sparkling cider and plastic champagne glasses.

My heart swells as I watch him set everything up with thoughtful and delicate care. I fight the urge to kiss him, but the more effort I see he's put into this, the harder it is to fight, and the less I want to. So, I lean over and gently place my soft lips against his. He moans at the contact and immediately stops what he's doing and slides his fingers through my hair to keep me close. I slowly pull away but keep my forehead resting against his, the connection both sweet and familiar.

He gazes at me tenderly. "What was that for?"

"For everything you do for me."

"I just want to make you happy." He seems so vulnerable when he says it. He has to know that I've never been happier than I have been these last several months with him.

"You do make me happy. So happy," I whisper before leaning in and kissing him again. This time the kiss gets deeper, our tongues sliding across each other before he pulls away.

His voice is hoarse when he speaks. "Let's eat before I totally lose control. I want this to be romantic for you."

"This?"

"Yeah, this." There's a weight to his last word, and he looks at me expectantly, desire and longing clear as day in his eyes. When he grabs my hand, turns it over, and gently kisses the inside of my wrist, a pulse of heat goes straight to my core like a bolt of lightning just struck my body.

"Oh."

This is happening. He brought me here so we could...we're going to...holy shit, I'm freaking out a little bit, but in the best way. I'm ready. I've been thinking about losing my virginity with Jack more times than I can count.

"Is this okay?" he asks, suddenly seeming unsure of himself.

I kiss him again before whispering, "It's perfect."

TEN

Jack

I'm way more nervous than I thought I'd be. I've heard all about sex in the locker room, and I've been endlessly hassled for not sealing the deal with Paige yet, but I didn't want to rush her. I didn't expect to feel so nervous, though. I've been thinking about this almost nonstop since we started dating, but not once did I think I'd be trembling, the knot in my stomach all nerves and excitement.

Paige is smiling with her eyes closed, her head pointed up toward the darkening sky. The sunset behind her outlines her silhouette with a soft glow, and I'm convinced she's never looked more beautiful than she does in this moment. She's breathtaking, and I can't believe this girl is really mine.

My chest hurts at the thought that in one short month, I won't get to see her every day. It feels so unfair that I get this taste of heaven for six months, and then it's going to get taken from me.

Okay, maybe that's a little dramatic. But still, I'm realistic enough to know that sixteen-year-olds can't usually make long-distance relationships work. I shake the thought from my head. I need to stop worrying about the future, especially when I have

Paige sitting right here looking more gorgeous than ever and she's all mine. I need to enjoy these moments while I still have them.

I slide my fingers through her silken brown hair. I'm mesmerized by her and endlessly fascinated with the feel of her soft strands as my fingers glide through them.

Her eyes still closed, she lets out a little sigh. "I love when you do that. It feels so good."

She opens her eyes slowly and turns to me, giving me that look I know is reserved for only me. I've never seen her look at anyone else like this, and I don't ever want to—I think it would kill me to watch her look at another guy this way. I don't know what I did to deserve her, but in this moment, I want to kiss the ground she walks on. Instead, I lean in and kiss her perfectly luscious and tempting pink lips until she parts them on a moan and allows me to deepen the kiss.

Without breaking our kiss, I gently lay her back on the few blankets we're sitting on and cover her body with mine, so I'm positioned between her legs. Even with all our clothes on, it's my new favorite place to be. The feel of her beneath me, her hands in my short brown hair, her breathy moans, and the slide of her tongue against mine is unreal. I pull back and look into her deep brown eyes that are now quickly filling with tears.

I catch an escaped tear with my thumb as I ask, "Paige, what's wrong?"

Did I move too fast? We've talked about this a lot. I thought she was ready, but now I'm worried I misunderstood things. I don't want to push her.

"Is this too fast? We can stop. I'm sorry, I thought—"

She cuts me off with a kiss. "I don't want to leave you," she whispers, anguish seeping into every word. It kills me that I can't fix this, that I can't make this better and take away her pain. Our pain.

"Shh. Don't think about that right now, okay? We'll figure it out. I love you, Paige. You're my best friend...my everything. We're going to get through this."

Paige reaches up to run her hands through my hair again and then pulls me down to her and kisses me softly.

"I love you so much, Jack." She kisses me deeper, her hands gripping my hair. "Make love to me."

I pull back. "Are you sure?"

She nods.

"I really need to hear you say it, Paige. I don't want to pressure you. We can wait."

"I don't want to wait. I'm sure. Stop talking and kiss me."

I can't deny Paige. I'd give her the whole world if I could. So I give her what she wants and lean down to kiss her softly, my lips trailing down to her collarbone. We've kissed like this before, but it feels different now, knowing that we're going all the way. She sits up a little and pulls off her shirt. We haven't seen anyone the entire time we've been here, but I still glance around to make sure we're out of sight and no one's around before reaching my hand around her back and fumbling with her bra hook.

God, I'm so nervous my hands are trembling. I want this to be good for her. I know it'll probably be over way too fast because I'm sure she's going to feel amazing, but I want her to enjoy this. When I finally get her bra unhooked, I slide the straps down, not breaking eye contact with her. Paige has an incredible body, one I've spent many nights exploring in as many ways as I could, but I want her to know I'm looking at her, not just her body. This isn't just sex to me. This means something, and maybe I need to give up my guy card for feeling that way, but it is what it is.

She slides her fingers under my shirt, the contact causing goosebumps to break out along my flesh. I love when she touches me like this. It's not tentative or shy, but focused, seductive, like she's tracing every part of me and committing it to memory. As her hand explores my abs, I start hastily undoing the buttons of my shirt and then rip it off until we're lying there topless, skin on skin.

Nothing has ever felt better in my entire life.

I kiss her again, my mouth eager to join with hers, before moving down to unbutton her jeans. She helps by sliding them off while I slip out of my own. I pull a condom out of the basket —I came prepared—and set it down next to us, so I don't have to look for it later.

When I glance back at Paige, I see her laid out before me absolutely, unreservedly, perfectly naked. As much as we've hooked up the past few months, we've never been completely naked with each other. I take back everything I said about Paige being gorgeous before. She is, but damn, looking at her spread out like this—I've never seen anyone or anything so beautiful in my entire life. I can hardly speak, I'm in such awe of her.

Our hands explore each other, our lips sometimes following. I'm not usually such a touchy-feely kind of guy, but this moment is everything I hoped it would be, not just for Paige but also for me. We fumble around with the condom as I try desperately to remember the lessons about safe sex from health class. It doesn't help that I've never been this hard in my life, and every touch makes my dick twitch with a raw need I've never felt before. She lets out a laugh as she watches me struggle, which pulls me from my own nerves and settles my shaking hands. Once it's on, I focus back on her, and the laughter fades as I use my fingers to feel her warm, wet heat and make sure she's prepared for me.

But it's the sight of my body slowly sliding into hers that will be forever burned in my memory.

Oh. Fuck. Me.

She's so tight.

It's the most unbelievable feeling in the world, and I have to stop for a second, taking deep breaths and closing my eyes. I'm praying for the control to make this last because I desperately want this to be as good for her as it currently feels for me. I glance down and realize I'm not even in that far. Jesus Christ, I might die from pleasure if this is how good she feels when I'm barely inside. With one more deep breath, I feel under control enough to keep pushing deeper. She inhales sharply, and I stop.

"Does it hurt?"

"A little." She takes a deep breath. "Just keep going."

"Maybe we should stop."

I'm pretty sure it would kill me at this point, but I can't hurt Paige. I start to slide out, but she grabs my ass and holds me to her.

Her gaze is pleading, her mouth a breath away from mine. "Don't stop, Jack. It's okay. It's normal for it to hurt the first time. It'll go away. Please don't stop. I want you to be my first."

Like I said before, I can't deny Paige anything. I take a steadying breath and continue to push into her. I push a little harder and finally settle my now painfully hard dick fully inside her. She cries out, then closes her eyes and takes a deep breath. I want to stop—I mean, I don't want to because this feels fucking incredible, but at the same time, I can't stand the idea of Paige in pain, while all I feel is pleasure. I'm just about to pull out and tell her we can try again another time, but then I feel her squeeze around me and I'm lost in the ecstasy of this moment.

She opens her eyes, her brown gaze locking with mine, and whispers, "Don't stop, Jack." So, I keep going. I slowly pump in and out of her, and I'm like ninety-nine point nine percent sure that I could die of total bliss right now. She feels so fucking good. The pleasure shoots through me, nearly overwhelming me. As I feel my body start to lose control, I realize I'm not going to last much longer. Not with how tightly she's gripping me, or the way she's moaning and writhing underneath me.

Despite my struggle for control, I know enough from locker room talk that I want her to come first. The guys have talked about all different methods to hold off, so I start reciting the alphabet backward in my head, but I get distracted by the noises she's making. They sound different than earlier.

"Does it feel good?"

"Yes," she whispers.

Her eyes meet mine, and I'm completely lost to her. If Paige didn't have all of me before, she sure as shit does now.

I continue to pump inside her, but I'm losing my battle for control.

"Paige, I can't hold off much longer. You feel so fucking good. Too good."

My muscles are tight and burning from the restraint. My whole body is fraught with tension. She's moaning more now, and the only thought in my head is that I need to make her come.

I suddenly remember something my teammate, Brandon Fishell, told me about rubbing a girl's clit to make her come. I move one of my hands down toward her clit—a part of her anatomy I have memorized over the past few months since we started hooking up—and start rubbing it gently. Her gorgeous chocolate-brown eyes widen, her breath stutters, and she lets out the sexiest moan I've ever heard as her body gyrates against mine, wholly lost to the feeling. It's so sexy. Suddenly, she tightens and pulses around me as she calls out my name, her arms scraping down my back as ecstasy washes across her face. The feel of her coming around me is my undoing, and I completely lose it. I come hard—harder than I ever thought was possible. So hard, I have a tiny moment of panic that I broke the condom because there's no way it could hold up against an orgasm that powerful. Thankfully, when I pull out, I notice the condom is still intact.

We lie there on our blankets, holding each other for a long time after, not talking but just staring up at the sky as the sun fades along the horizon. I'm playing with Paige's hair, holding her tightly to me, her hand wrapped around my waist, another blanket covering our naked bodies and protecting us from the chill of the evening air.

"Was it okay?" I ask tentatively.

I want more than anything for her to have enjoyed it. I know I did.

She sits up and looks at me. "Jack, it was perfect."

A smile breaks across her face, and I let out a relieved breath. I pull her back down to me, holding her close.

I never want to leave this moment.

I kiss her hair and tell her how much I love her, even though those words don't feel strong enough to convey how I feel about her. I know now, without a doubt, that Paige is it for me. She's the only one who will ever make me feel like this. She has all of me, heart, body, and soul.

ELEVEN

Paige

I don't know how long we lie together, our naked bodies touching, Jack's hand running through my hair. In this moment, I know without a doubt that he owns all of me, and there will never be anyone else for me. I love him beyond words, especially because he made this night everything I ever hoped it would be and so much more. If I didn't have the move to Chicago looming over my head, I'd be one hundred percent sure that Jack and I would end up married someday. But the reality is we are moving.

I don't look at him when I start talking. I can't.

"We need to talk about what'll happen when I move to Chicago." I don't mean to whisper the words, but that's how they come out anyway.

He exhales heavily. "I know." He sounds so sad and defeated, and I hate this position that we've found ourselves in.

"Do you think we can make it work?" It's the question I've been asking myself nonstop. Truthfully, I'm afraid of his answer because I'm worried he'll say no.

"I don't know," he whispers.

He kisses my forehead softly. "Paige, I love you with every

ounce of my being. But we're sixteen. You're moving over two thousand miles away, and neither of us has a job, so it's not like we can pay for trips to see each other without our parents' help. I want to believe we can make this work long distance, but I just don't know. The longest we've been apart was two months last summer, and it sucked. And that was before we were even a couple. We haven't been apart at all since we started dating, and the idea of being separated from you kills me."

"It kills me too. But can't we at least try?"

He looks at me sharply then exclaims, "Of course we're going to fucking try! Did you honestly think I was telling you we should break up?"

I shrug. "Kinda. I mean, you sound so defeated. It sounded like you were already resigned to it not working out."

"Paige, the odds aren't on our side, that's for sure. But there's no one else in the world I want to be with. I will fight for us. It won't be easy, not on either of us, but we're definitely going to try to make it work. I'm not giving you up that easily."

"I'll fight for us too. I'm not giving you up, either."

I kiss him deeply, once again lost in the feel of his mouth on mine. It's dark now, and I know we should head back home, but I don't want to leave. Being with Jack like this is my definition of perfection. It's my happy place, and if I could stay here forever, I would.

The next few weeks fly by. Jack and I spend every minute together that we can and take advantage of his parents being gone at several events when we're supposed to be studying.

Jack is so attentive to my needs when we're together. I now understand how people can get addicted to sex. I crave the feel of Jack almost constantly, especially when it seems like sex gets better every time. We've become so familiar with each other's bodies that I'm pretty sure I know his as well as I know my own.

This last week has been different, though. There's almost an urgency when we're together—like we can't get enough of each other to sate this need that's clawing at us both. We haven't talked about it, but I know what's driving it. I move on Friday.

We've both been denying the inevitable for far too long. It's time to come up with a plan. We're lying together on his bed, barely covered by his sheet. My hand is drawing circles on his chest, and I can't take the silence anymore.

"Jack, we should talk about what's happening in two days."

He immediately sits up and swings his feet off the side of the bed. He pushes off and starts getting dressed, as dread fills my gut.

I sit up, covering myself with his sheet. "Jack."

Without looking at me, he says, "I don't want to talk about it. We should probably study for the test tomorrow anyway."

"Jack, I couldn't care less about that test. I leave on Friday. As in, two days from now. We've hardly talked about it."

"What's there to talk about?"

My heart lodges in my throat, but I push it down and try to stay focused instead of feeling hurt and worried by his words. "Are you serious right now? How about figuring out how things are going to work? Are we going to call each other every night? Are you going to come out to visit before you have to go to football camp, or am I coming back here? We should make a plan, so we have something to look forward to."

He turns to me sharply, his mouth in an angry snarl and his gaze furious. "Something to look forward to? I'm supposed to be excited about having to wait several months before seeing my girlfriend again? Fuck that."

His anger surprises me. He was sad and defeated before about the move, but never angry. I realize I'm still sitting here naked, while he's now standing fully clothed, his arms crossed and his body language completely closed off. I've never felt so vulnerable or exposed with Jack before, but I do now.

I get up and quickly get dressed while my heart plummets to my stomach. I can't stop the silent tears streaming down my face. This wasn't what I wanted. I thought it would be easier if we knew exactly when we'd get to see each other again. It wouldn't make our situation feel so desolate.

Apparently, Jack doesn't see things that way. I can't tell if he's angry with me or with the situation, or maybe both, but I can't help feeling hurt. His reaction scares me because this is what I've been afraid of all along. That he'd want to give up and break up.

I speak softly. "You said you'd fight for us. We said we'd fight for each other. That's all I wanted."

There's a tremor in my voice that I wish he didn't hear, but by the look he gives me, I can tell he did. His eyes lose their anger and quickly fill with remorse and sadness.

"I'm sorry, Paige." He runs his fingers through his hair in frustration. "I can't stand the idea of you leaving. I've tried to push it out of my mind."

"You can't ignore it for much longer, you know."

"I know."

The defeat and heartache in his tone match how I feel. I don't know what to say to make this better or easier for us. We're at an impasse, and I'm no longer confident that we'll make it out the other side unscathed.

TWELVE

Jack

This is the day I've been dreading for a month. My parents let me skip school, so I could be with Paige until her family leaves. I've hardly talked to her since the other night when she wanted us to make a plan. I know her feelings were hurt, but I'm having a hard time too. The last thing I wanted to do was ruin what little time we had left talking about how long it'll be before we see each other again. But there's no avoiding it now.

The U-Haul is packed up, and her parents are doing their final walk-through of their empty house. Paige and I have been sitting on the back porch steps holding hands for the last half hour, not saying a word. There's so much I want to say, and yet I can't find the words. It's the most confusing feeling I've ever experienced, and I hate this helpless ache that's permeating my entire body.

Her dad comes out on the back porch. "Paige, honey. We're going to leave in about ten minutes, okay?"

She speaks quietly, dejectedly. "Okay, Dad."

He goes back inside, and each second ticks by like it's the last, the weight of what's coming bearing down on both of us until I feel like I'm being suffocated.

"I can't stand this," I murmur, and then I lean in and kiss her hard, desperate for this connection with her, for this one perfect moment where it's just the two of us and we can pretend our whole future isn't about to change. I twine my fingers in her hair and deepen the kiss.

Everything is right in the world when we're together. Why does she have to leave? I hate this so much. I pull away to look at her and see tears streaming down her face.

"I love you so much, Jack. Please don't give up on us. I need you."

I hold her close, not ready to let her go—I'm not sure I'll ever be ready to let her go. "I need you too. I won't give up. We'll make it work, okay? You'll call me as soon as you get to Chicago and then we'll start planning when we can see each other. I love you. It's all going to work out, okay?"

She nods, her eyes filled with despair and yet still hopeful that we can make this work. I kiss her again, sealing my promise to her that we will find a way to stay together. It won't be easy, but we can do this. We're meant to be together, that I know for sure.

We stand up, hands clasped together tightly, and I walk her out to the front. Everything is packed, and it feels so surreal, like this is happening to someone else and I'm just watching it. Except that my heart feels like each moment closer to her departure is another stab, and that pain feels very real. Seeing the tears streaming down her face and knowing she's struggling just as much makes this even harder. I turn her toward me and use my thumbs to brush her tears away.

"None of that, okay? This isn't goodbye forever. It's just goodbye for now."

I make sure she's looking me right in the eyes. "You're my best friend...my everything. Never forget that. You're stuck with me forever, okay?"

She takes a deep breath and nods. With one final kiss and a whispered "I love you," she's shuffled into the car, and they drive away. I stand there on their lawn, my arm held up in a frozen wave, until they round the corner.

That's when I lose it.

I sink to the grass, my arms draped across my bent knees, and hang my head. I can feel the tears as they stream down my face. I know I'm supposed to be tough and manly, but right now, I don't give a shit. I just had to watch the girl I love drive away to another state thousands of miles away, and I don't even know when we'll see each other again.

I realize now that Paige was right. We should've made a plan before she left. I feel gutted and empty—the painful pressure in my chest is immense. I've never felt this awful before.

I drive straight home and go to my room, not interested in talking to anyone. I know my parents saw me, but they have the decency to give me some space to sort through my feelings. My dad eventually knocks on my door to check on me, but I get him to leave me alone pretty quickly.

I'm lying on my bed, waiting for sleep to claim me when my phone dings with a text.

Paige: I miss you.

My chest constricts, and I feel that burning sensation in the back of my throat and eyes. God, I miss her so much already. I want to hold her more than anything else right now.

Me: I miss you too. Where are you guys? Did you stop for the night?

Paige: Yeah. We made it to Ogden, Utah. It's boring. We're getting up early to continue the drive, but I can't sleep.

Me: Me either.

Paige: We're going to get through this, right, Jack?

Me: Yeah. We'll get through this.

We have to get through this. I'm not sure I know how to live without Paige in my life.

PART 2: NOW

THIRTEEN

Paige

You know that feeling you have when you first wake up and notice that it's brighter than normal? That feeling just a split second before the panic sets in that it's too bright and you realize you're running late? That's the feeling I have when I shoot straight up in bed and reach for my alarm clock.

"Shit!" I say, adrenaline spiking through my veins as my heart races and drops to my stomach at the same time. I'm going to be late for my first day at the *LA Chronicle*.

I'm never late.

I dash out of bed like my ass is on fire. Frantically, I search for my clothes. Why the hell didn't my alarm go off? I swear, I set it.

Suddenly, blinding pain in my toe debilitates me. "Dammit!" I hop around on one foot, trying to hold in the other curses battling to get out of my mouth.

"Stupid boxes," I mumble, attempting to shove them aside. I've lived in this apartment for two days, and it's astoundingly clear that I've had no time to unpack anything. Half-full boxes litter my new six hundred square foot, one-bedroom apartment in downtown Los Angeles. It costs me a fortune to live downtown, but the commute is easy since my office is only one mile away. I couldn't stand the idea of being stuck on the freeway in the notoriously horrible LA traffic for hours at a time just trying to get to work. Plus, my new job at the *LA Chronicle* came with a pay raise. My old meager salary from when I worked at the *San Francisco Gazette* barely covered my cost of living.

I stumble into the shower—graceful as ever this morning—and quickly lather my body with soap. I'd skip it altogether since I'm already running exceptionally late, but I was too tired last night after my weak attempt to unpack. I can still feel the after-effects of moving—that grimy feeling of dried sweat and greasy hair. It's not a lovely image.

I quickly rinse my hair before running back into my room, tripping over another half-unpacked box in the process, and throwing on a modest black pencil skirt and white blouse. Not my nicest professional outfit, but I honestly don't know which box is holding most of my clothes. Yes, I was the moron who didn't pack them in suitcases or something to keep them separated from all my other household essentials, and who also failed to label any of my boxes—rookie move. I complete my ensemble with simple black flats since my toes have been tortured enough today, and then dash out the door.

I make it to the office only five minutes late, but that's still about twenty minutes later than I was hoping to be on my first day.

My job is my life—I'm the definition of a workaholic—and I pride myself on my work ethic. Running late is not the first impression I wanted to present to my new boss, who I've heard is a real ballbuster. Anxiety courses through me as I silently hope and pray that my tardiness doesn't start me off on the wrong foot when I had such high hopes of making an excellent first impression.

I hurry down the hall toward his office, double-checking the sign on the door before entering and seeing Vince Rosenburg, my new editor, sitting behind his desk. His dark hair has a bit of salt and pepper, but he still looks handsome for a man in his fifties. His glasses sit low on his nose, and when I enter he glances at me above the rim without ever moving his head up.

"Paige O'Malley." He pointedly looks at the clock on the wall across from him. "I was wondering when you were going to make your way into work."

I try to hide my subtle wince, but Vince is as shrewd as they come—a sign of a seasoned reporter and editor—and I can tell by the slight arch of his brow that he caught it.

"Have a seat. Let's talk about assignments."

"Yes, sir. I apologize for being late." I don't make excuses, since I don't have a good one, and I know it won't matter to him anyway. But I figure he'll respect the apology.

He may respect it, but he doesn't acknowledge it. "So, remind me what you did at the *Gazette* again?"

He and I both know that he is well aware of my work at the *Gazette*. I wouldn't be sitting in front of him if he didn't know my qualifications, but I'm guessing he's making me jump through extra hoops due to my tardiness. I decide it's best to play along.

"I've done a little bit of everything. The *Gazette* was great about allowing reporters to cover every area of the paper before selecting which section to focus on. My favorite assignments were the features and local news. My portfolio included several of my recent pieces."

He pulls out my portfolio from under a stack of papers on the corner of his desk. "Yes, I've looked over it. I noticed you did some sports writing as well."

"Yes, but I didn't feel very qualified to cover sports—I'm not a huge sports fan," I confess. That's not entirely true, but the truth is complicated and something I rarely share with people.

"You don't have to be a fan to write it well, which you did," he says, his sharp penetrating gaze spearing me to my seat with its intensity. He looks back at my portfolio. "I was especially impressed with your football coverage and your personal profile piece on the mayor. I'd be curious to see you tie the two areas together."

"I'm not sure I follow you..."

He leans back in his chair, folding his hands over his slightly protruding belly. "There's a lot of talk that the Los Angeles Wolves could go all the way to the Super Bowl this year. The team is better than ever, especially now that it's led by the best quarterback in the NFL. Do you know anything about Jack Fuller?"

My heart plummets to my stomach. That's such a loaded question, but there's no way he could possibly know my history with Jack.

Of course, I knew Jack was in LA, but I didn't think our paths would ever cross. There are over three million people in Los Angeles.

How can I diplomatically get out of this assignment if my boss is going where I think he's going? I can't see Jack again. I'm not ready. I don't know if I'll ever be ready, not after how things ended. Not after he shattered my heart and made me feel like I meant nothing to him.

"Um, I don't know too much. Like I said before, sports coverage wasn't my forte. I was mainly a features and local news writer. The only thing I've ever heard about him is that he never gives any personal interviews."

That is a blatant lie, which makes me feel a little queasy because I hate lying, but I'm also not about to share that Jack and I have a long, complicated history. Or the fact that I've followed Jack's career ever since college.

"Exactly!" My boss leans forward excitedly. "I want you to

be the reporter that gets a personal interview. You did incredible work on your human-interest pieces, and you have sports in your background. Even if it's not strong, it doesn't matter since the focus will be on Jack and his private life. He never gives anybody more than he has to at those damn press conferences. It'd be one hell of a story if we could get him to talk to us."

Panic surges inside me, but my face remains passive and my tone neutral as I ask, "Why me? Surely there have to be other reporters more qualified..."

"You don't want it? Half my reporters would die for this opportunity. Jack Fuller is hot right now, and I want coverage on him while people still care. Why wouldn't you take this opportunity?"

He looks at me curiously, and I squirm in my seat. He's right. It would be an incredible opportunity to get the most notoriously private quarterback in the league to give a personal interview, which is something he's never done before. But I just can't be the person that does it. Vince would never understand, but when it comes to Jack, I need to keep my distance. Moving to LA to work for such an esteemed paper was too good an opportunity to pass up, but I have no desire to ever see the man who broke my heart into a million pieces again.

"I'm sorry, sir, I just don't think I'm the right person for this piece. But I'd be happy to do another assignment. In fact, I have several ideas about some stories that would be—"

He cuts me off. "Maybe I wasn't clear. I'm putting you on sports. I hired you for a specific reason."

My eyes widen. "Excuse me?"

He stands and walks around his desk, leaning on the front in a classic move of power intimidation. "I did a little digging into your past, specifically the fact that you went to high school with Jack. You must know each other."

My chest constricts as though there's no oxygen in the room.

He continues, "Getting a personal interview—the first of its kind out of this guy—would set this paper apart from all the other news affiliates that have tried. Most quarterbacks love the limelight, but not Fuller. I want to be the paper that gets that interview out of him before someone else manages to do it." He gives me a stern look. "You *will* take this assignment, or you can go back to San Francisco, if they'll even take you back. You know how quickly those positions get snatched up."

I stare at him, too shocked to speak right away. I knew he was ruthless, but I never saw this coming.

I can't lose this job. Working for a major paper like the *Chronicle* has been my dream since college. Jack has taken enough from me—I won't let him take this too.

"I'll do it."

Vince gives me a condescending smirk. "I knew you'd change your mind."

It's been nine years since I've seen or talked to Jack Fuller. The last time I saw him was when he walked away from me at Chicago's O'Hare airport when we were seventeen. He broke up with me via text once he got home. A fucking text message, like everything we'd ever had meant absolutely nothing. I'm ashamed to admit that I begged him to call me before raging at him for being a coward.

No one has ever hurt me the way he did. I've never let any other man get that close.

After gathering my press credentials, I head out to my car to go to the stadium since Vince wants me to start working on this immediately. My breathing gets heavier the closer I get to my car. My chest gets tight, my pulse pounds in my ears, and my airways start to feel constricted as a panic attack grips me.

Oh God. Not now. Come on, body, I need you to work with me here. I need to be strong, not weak.

I quickly press speed dial for my best friend, Gina Rodrigo, knowing if anyone can help talk me down from my panic, it's her. Gina has talked or held me through several since we became friends during our freshman year of college, although it's been years since I had one. She'll be able to help me get through this. I hope.

She picks up on the third ring. "Hey, girl, how's sunny SoCal?"

I cut right to the chase because I'm now officially struggling to breathe. "My editor assigned me to interview Jack." Gina knows all about my history with Jack and how brokenhearted I was when he dumped me.

"Oh shit." Her tone is hushed and serious. "Are you okay? What the hell am I asking? Of course you're not okay. You're freaking out right now, aren't you?"

I make an affirmative sound as tears fill my eyes, sweat builds on my neck and hairline, and my hands start to shake, my body officially working against me.

"Okay. Deep breaths. Close your eyes and do 5-2-5. I'll count. Breathe in for one, two, three, four, five. Now hold, one, two, and breathe out, two, three, four, five." I follow the soothing calm of her voice and do the breathing exercise she found online a few years ago three more times before my trembling subsides and my heart rate slows. Once again, I'm immensely thankful that fate brought her into my life.

Gina is a features writer for the *Gazette*. We met in college and became instant best friends. She was actually the one who helped me get my job in San Francisco. I'd been working at a small paper near Chicago but needed a change of scenery. I missed the west coast and Gina knew it. She's confident and fierce—a total force to be reckoned with. Gina says it comes from the fact that she's from a huge Puerto Rican family where she learned to be loud if she wanted her opinions to be heard. Either way, she's been a godsend in my life.

"How you doin' now?" she asks, her voice still soft and low.

"Better. I think the worst of it is over." My chest still aches, but the rest of my body is coming down from the panic, my muscles no longer clenched.

"Paige, you can handle this. You're not that seventeen-year-old girl anymore. You're a kick-ass writer for the *LA* freaking *Chronicle*! Go out and show that man what he missed out on! You're smoking hot, girl. Let him see what he could've had. He'll regret the day he let you go, I guaran-fucking-tee it."

I take another deep breath, hoping it can also bolster my faltering confidence. "You're right. You're absolutely right. I can do this. It's no big deal." I attempt to sound nonchalant.

"Well, I mean, it's kinda a big deal..."

Okay, not helpful. "Gina!"

"But," she emphasizes the word, "you're going to rock the interview."

"Except for the fact that he's notorious for not doing personal interviews. Why would he

talk to me? Because we dated for like a second nine years ago? That's ridiculous."

"First of all, you dated for almost a year, not a second, and you were best friends for over ten years before that. He'd be crazy not to talk to you."

"I love and appreciate your optimism, but if Jack wanted to talk to me, he had plenty of time to do so."

And that's another nail in the coffin that is my history with Jack. He's never once spoken to me since he sent that text breaking up with me nine years ago. Not a text, not a call, not even a fucking messenger pigeon. Nothing. Radio silence from the man who used to know me better than I sometimes knew myself. The pain of that is still more acute than I'd like for it to be, although I've buried it as deep as I can.

I learned a long time ago that his silence was louder than any words could ever be.

Jack Fuller is just an assignment. That's how I have to look at this. He can't be anything more.

He gave up his chance a long time ago.

FOURTEEN

Jack

I wipe the sweat from my brow, my body exhausted from another grueling practice. People may think that athletes have it easy—we get paid millions to play a sport for a living—but there's nothing easy about the intensive diet and workout regimen or punishing practices we go through. I'm looking forward to relaxing tonight before our big game tomorrow.

I head over to the sidelines where I see Max Donnelly, my best friend and assistant. My agent thought it wouldn't hurt to have an assistant—someone I trusted—to field all the crazy requests I get for interviews, parties, etc. As soon as he made the suggestion, Max popped into my head.

Max and I were roommates our freshman year of college. We bonded immediately, and in the years since he's become more like my brother. He's seen me during some of the darkest moments of my life. The times where memories of a future I threw away would plague me until I was convinced I'd feel less pain if someone just ripped my heart straight from my body.

He's always had my back, and now I pay him a pretty penny to basically deal with all the shit I don't want to. He doesn't seem to mind, and it means we get to hang out daily. It's a pretty sweet setup. Plus, there weren't too many people I trusted to take the position—one that required knowing a lot about my personal life.

I learned early on in my career to keep my life private. I'll do the standard postgame press conferences, but I never let them touch my personal life. I have Kallie to thank for that. My college girlfriend became jealous of my dedication to football and decided to cheat on me during the biggest championship weekend of my college career—with my teammate of all people. Pictures of them got out, and suddenly the press barely cared that we'd won the Lemon Cup. All they could talk about was the star quarterback getting cheated on. It took months for the scandal to die down, and by the time it did, I was more determined than ever that the media would never get anything personal out of me again.

Max approaches me with a smug grin on his face. "Another reporter came snooping around for you. She was hot."

I laugh loudly. "Another woman? Man, these papers are desperate to get an interview out of me. What's that, the third one this week? As if I'd change all my beliefs because they send a woman instead of a man. Get outta here with that noise. Why can't they just let it go? I'm a private guy. Why can't they respect that I want to keep it that way? There are plenty of other guys in the league they could focus on."

I may have started out laughing, but my frustration is pretty clear by the end of my rant. It's been a sticking point with me for a long time—journalists are fucking vultures. Growing up with a high-profile lawyer for a dad, he made sure I understood the value of maintaining my privacy. The scandal with Kallie in college only reinforced that idea. But for some fucked-up reason, me saying "No" seems to imply to the media that they simply aren't trying hard enough. All these journalists think that my refusal really just means I haven't been offered the right price. The truth is, there is no right price.

My agent, Dan, has told me time and time again that this is the price I pay for being in the public eye, for being the NFL's golden boy and star quarterback. Dan thinks I should just play along and they'll all settle down. He doesn't understand my hesitation, no matter how many times I've tried to explain it to him these past five years.

My private life, while boring these days, is the only thing that's mine. I love football more than anything else in my life. It's been that way since I was seventeen, when I threw all my focus into it after shattering my own heart. Loneliness and grief can be powerful motivators. Football was the only thing that helped me bury my feelings.

All that being said, football has become something I do for other people as much as I do it for myself, but it's not solely mine. My private life is. Nobody is in charge of it except for me.

I can understand why people struggle to grasp where I'm coming from—most think I'm hiding something, which I'm not. The reality is it's hard to explain unless you're in my shoes.

Max pulls me out of my head. "Don't worry, man. I sent her away. I got your back, brother. You know that."

I just shake my head, murmur a quick "thank you," and then head to the showers. Max knows better than anyone how much my privacy means to me. He's the kid of a famous rock star, and his whole childhood was splashed across the media. He was also around for the Kallie mess. He gets it. I'm never more thankful for him than I am in moments like this.

After a quick shower and change, I get in my car and head home but am almost immediately stopped by bumper-to-bumper traffic. The traffic in LA is the goddamn worst. It has become the bane of my existence since I moved here, but normally I just shrug it off and deal with it. Lately, I've been feeling antsy and easily irritable. I think the pressure I've put on myself, and that others have put on me, is starting to get to me.

I need a distraction, something to get me out of this headspace I seem to find myself in more and more frequently these days. I consider calling one of the many women in my phone who I know would be up for a quick fuck. That usually helps release some of the tension, albeit temporarily. I pull my phone out of my pocket—since traffic is at a complete standstill—prepared to dial the first name that I come across in my contacts. I take a moment to glance out my dark-tinted windows—looking out at the world from this safe space—and notice a brunette a few cars over, her hair falling in soft waves around her shoulders, her eyes hidden by sunglasses, and her lips moving as if she's singing to her radio. My whole body tenses, my chest aches, and the loneliness I work so hard to keep buried bubbles up immediately. I can't see the woman's face, but she looks so much like Paige from this angle, I almost believe it's her.

I fight against the emotions trying to claw their way through my body as memories of Paige slam into me piece by piece until I feel nearly breathless from how much I still miss her. I ruined my chances with Paige a long time ago. Still, I'm rattled enough that the idea of being with another woman right now makes me feel sick. I put my phone back in my pocket and lose myself in my memories.

Paige was my first and only love. Every woman since her has paled in comparison to the radiant ray of light that Paige brought into my life. I've always regretted breaking up with her, and in the past few years, I've accepted that she was the one that got away, or more like the one I drove away by breaking her heart like what we had meant nothing. I should've fought for her, but I was young, and the long distance felt like never-ending torture.

I've checked up on her on social media during moments of

weakness—many, many moments, if I'm being honest with myself—almost always after I've had a few drinks and I'm sitting at home late at night.

The longest I've been able to go without checking her social media accounts was six months, and that was only after I saw her post a picture with another guy. I was so filled with jealousy that I ended up drinking an entire fifth of whiskey that night, trying to bury the feelings I had no right to have. I'd given her up. She deserved to find happiness. But I couldn't stay away long and eventually caved and checked her profile again. The guy was no longer in the picture by that time.

I know I have no right to be jealous of her dating. I've dated plenty of other women, but they were always just my attempts to replace Paige. Hell, even Kallie knew she was just a placeholder.

It took me six years before I finally accepted that Paige was irreplaceable. She was one of a kind, and I'd been the asshole who let her go. But as much as I miss the hell out of her, I was always so ashamed about how I ended things that I haven't had the guts to contact her. I figured if she had forgiven me, then she'd have reached out to me. Now I can't help but wonder if I've once again taken the coward's way out with her. Maybe she's been waiting for me to contact her. Would she even talk to me? I doubt it.

I've spent the last three years working hard to accept that our time has passed, and I need to find a way to move on—*really* move on. I figure once my stubborn heart can accept that, then it'll finally let me love someone else.

I really thought I'd be further in my life. I mean, I have a great job, make a shitload of money, have a huge house, and can have any woman I want—except for the one woman I really want. But I thought that by now that huge house would be filled with a family—my family. I thought I'd have a wife and maybe even a kid.

I know I'm only twenty-six, but with my thirtieth birthday looming closer every day—and the reality that I'm still hung up on a woman I let go of nine years ago—I've been thinking a lot about my future and reassessing what I want. I only have maybe five to ten good years left in football, providing I don't get injured. But what will I have after football?

My deep-seated desire for privacy has made me feel more isolated than ever, and I can't help but wonder if football has been worth the sacrifice. At the end of the day, what's the point of life if you have no one to share it with? If you don't have anyone who really knows you?

After sitting in traffic for two hours and being stuck with my thoughts, I finally make it home to my huge, empty house. I take a deep breath and head straight for the kitchen, where I pour myself a glass of whiskey. I can't get drunk since I have a game tomorrow, but I can try to ease this ever-present ache in my chest. I lose myself in some game tape in order to prep myself for tomorrow. By eleven, I shuffle off to bed and fall into a fitful night's sleep, thinking that maybe, just maybe, tomorrow will be better.

FIFTEEN

Paige

"I didn't get to interview him. His stupid assistant wouldn't even let me past security when I stopped by practice yesterday. Then I got stuck in horrible traffic trying to get home from the stadium. Have I mentioned lately how much I hate traffic in LA?" I whine as I finish my rant to Gina during our phone call.

"You've only mentioned the horrible traffic like a million times. Don't forget, I grew up in Long Beach. I totally get how bad the traffic is in that area. Let's focus on the bigger issue. Are you really ready to see Jack again?"

I stare out the window of my apartment, watching the bustling people and cars of downtown. "I don't really have a choice, do I? I won't let him ruin the career I've worked so hard for, and if this is the only way to prove to Vince that I was worth hiring, then I have to do it. The bigger question is will he even talk to me?"

"Do you really think he'd blow you off?"

"I don't know. I don't know him anymore, if I ever really knew him to begin with."

"Don't do that," she scolds, as she always does when my thoughts stray this direction. "You knew him. I've heard your story, and there's no way that boy didn't love the shit out of you. But we all do stupid shit when we're young. His stupid shit was dumping you via text message, and I'd bet a million dollars that he regrets that decision."

"It doesn't matter. I just need to find a way to convince him to sit down and let me interview him."

"That simple, huh?" I can hear her calling my bluff.

No, it's not that simple. It's never been that simple. I've carried the wounds of our breakup for far longer than I want to admit. What twenty-six-year-old woman is still hung up on her first love? I should be stronger than this.

And most days I feel like I am. But most days, I'm also not forced to figure out how I'm going to conduct an interview with the last man on earth I even want to be in a room with.

"I'm scared," I whisper, my voice catching.

"Of what?" Gina asks, her tone turning gentle.

How can I possibly explain all the complex emotions swirling inside me? I've spent so long trying to bury these feelings, that now that they're swirling up uncontrollably, I'm lost and overwhelmed trying to process them all at once.

I'd convinced myself I would never see him again, but now that I will be, I'm terrified of what that interaction will look like. I don't know if I'm more afraid of him having no reaction to me at all or him reacting to me the same way I've always reacted to him. Everything we felt about each other was so strong and intense. I've never been able to replicate those feelings or even feel something remotely close since. In fact, I've found myself in a string of shitty relationships with guys who continually made me feel unworthy. I may be laser-focused and incredibly adept at my job, but my relationships have all ended as disasters. And after each disastrous ending, I've picked myself up, dusted myself off, and refocused on my career.

Jack has always been a weak spot for me. One I've hidden well, but a weak spot nonetheless.

"Hello, Paige? Scared of what?"

I'm pulled out my reverie. "Sorry. I zoned out. It's complicated and confusing. I don't really want to talk about this anymore. I need to get ready to go. I got a press pass for the game tonight. I'm hoping I might get close enough where I'll see him and I can ask him a couple of questions."

"Good luck. Call me if you start to panic. You know I've always got your back."

"I know. Thanks, Gina. Talk to you later."

We hang up, and I go to my closet, which I finally unpacked when I got home last night. I have no idea what to wear since I've never covered sports this seriously before. All my previous sports coverage consisted of college football games. They were pretty lax on professional dress expectations. Is professional football different? Probably.

I decide on a pair of black skinny jeans with a white blouse with frilly cap sleeves that reminds me of something I'd seen Erin Andrews wearing at a game I watched on TV once. I pair the ensemble with black boots and a black pendant necklace. It's comfortable, stylish, and professional without being a suit.

Knowing I'm going to see Jack tonight has me extra motivated to look my best. I spend twice as much time doing my hair and makeup than I normally do, but I don't care. I need to look composed and confident, even if those are the last two things I'm feeling right now.

The drive to the stadium takes less time than I hoped. Of course, the only time I want LA traffic, it's conveniently light. I make it to my seat fairly quickly and am not surprised that I'm practically right on the field. I could almost touch the players if they came over to me. Vince got me a close seat so I could focus on Jack and hopefully grab his attention, something I definitely wouldn't be able to do if I was in the press box. I have a press badge in my purse for the postgame interviews, which are usually held in the locker rooms or a room nearby.

The players come out, and the excitement in the stadium is palpable. Fans are already cheering, and the game hasn't even started yet. The Wolves fans are an impressive bunch and were recently named the loudest and most loyal fans in the league.

I see Jack run onto the field and my heart nearly stops.

He looks incredible. He's smiling and waving at the fans while I slide lower in my seat,

trying to hide behind those sitting near me. He's filled out so much more since high school, and the pictures I've seen simply don't do him justice.

My chest feels tight, and I can barely get breath in my lungs as I'm hit with a metaphorical two-ton truck.

His carefree smile and bright blue eyes instantly transport me back to that heartbroken girl who sat on her bed sobbing as she stared at her phone desperately praying for him to call or text her saying he made a huge mistake and he's an idiot. All the pain and hurt I've carried comes barreling over me, until anger shoves its way through. That call I was so desperate for never came. He never tried to fix it. He never tried at all.

Resolve pushes away my momentary panic, and I sit up in my seat, my eyes glued to his tall frame as he moves around the sidelines.

The game starts and I watch, enraptured by his commanding presence on the field. For a moment, I lose myself in watching him, mesmerized by the way his muscles move, his incredible precision on the field, the accuracy of his throws, and his quick and deliberate footwork. He's a machine on the gridiron and incredibly focused. It's clear that he's passionate about his job. I always found that attractive—how much he loved football. Obviously, his love and focus have only gotten stronger since the last time I saw him.

By the second quarter, it's a close game. The defense for the opposing team is insane and they've made their target clear—Jack. He's taken hit after hit, but the Wolves have still managed to lead by seven. They set up for their next play and start to run it.

I watch Jack as he shoots toward my side of the field. He's going to run right by me, and my heart leaps up into my throat at the idea of being that close to him. I'm distracted by watching him come closer and closer to where I'm sitting, so I don't notice the defensive linebacker until he smacks into Jack and slams him down to the ground.

I'm standing up and screaming his name before my brain processes the movement. I watch his head turn in my direction slowly. His eyes narrow and then he turns his head quickly to the sky. My heart is beating so hard I can hear it in my ears. I watch the coaches, trainers, and medics run out onto the field to check him. They're talking to him and he's moving his hands, but he still hasn't gotten up.

After what feels like an eternity but is probably only a few minutes, they help him sit up slowly and he takes off his helmet. I watch as he pushes his fingers through his hair and talks to the medics, although he's not looking at them but instead looking down at the ground. He seems to take a deep breath before turning his head in my direction.

Our gazes connect, and suddenly the rest of the stadium doesn't exist. His eyes always did suck me in. My breath freezes in my chest as I watch an array of varying emotions cross his face—disbelief, confusion, fear, and then what I'm afraid to believe is joy. A smile breaks out across his face, and with that simple movement I feel like I can finally breathe again.

He's okay. He's not hurt.

Thank God.

I hate that I care, but I do.

The medics help him up and escort him off the field to follow concussion protocol since he took such a hard hit. He doesn't look at me again until just before he reaches the tunnel, where he stops and turns his head back toward me. His face is blank this time, his emotions masked from me, before he turns around and disappears from my sight.

I drop back to my seat, reeling from what just happened.

I saw him.

He definitely saw me.

And two things are abundantly clear to me. Jack Fuller is still my kryptonite. And those old feelings I've always carried for him weren't buried as deep as I thought they were.

SIXTEEN

Jack

I replay the moment of the tackle in my head again, trying to sort through everything that just happened, while I sit in the locker room waiting for Max.

I was on the field, running the ball myself since none of my receivers were open, when out of nowhere, #96 barreled into me like a damn stampeding rhino. I hit the ground hard, banging my head against the field and causing me to see flashing stars in my vision.

That's when I heard it—or, more accurately, *her*.

I heard my name crystal clear—in her voice—and turned my head to see Paige with that same worried look she always had when she came to my games in high school and watched me get hit.

But it couldn't be her. Paige wasn't in my life anymore. And she definitely wouldn't be in the stands watching me play, although I've dreamed of that very thing more times than I can count.

I turned back and looked at the sky, blinking hard and trying to focus. I had to be hallucinating, but God, what a hallucination it had been. She looked so real and so good, I ached to hold her. My emotions were getting out of hand if I was starting to hallucinate images of Paige now.

The medics, trainers, and coaches crowded around me, asking me the standard questions to check if I was okay. The medics helped me sit up, but I kept my eyes focused on the ground, afraid that if I looked up, she wouldn't be there. I needed to pull myself together and realize that it was just my mind's wishful thinking. I must've been hit harder than I thought. I didn't think I had a concussion, but hallucinations could be a symptom, right?

When I looked up, I was prepared—well, at least bracing myself to be prepared—for her to not actually be there. But she was there, holding her hands in front of her mouth, fear on her face. Her eyes met mine, and for the first time since I walked away from her at the airport in Chicago, everything felt right in the world. It was like a lock clicking into place. She was really here.

Paige. My Paige.

I couldn't help the small smile that lifted my lips. I focused back on the medics who wanted to follow concussion protocol and take me into the locker room to be looked over. They helped me off the field, but I couldn't stop myself from looking back once more. When I turned back toward the tunnel, I was more determined than ever to make things right. Seeing her confirmed everything I'd been feeling. I've never gotten over Paige, but more importantly, I never would, and I needed to win her back.

Max runs into the room. "Man, are you okay? That was one hell of a hit. How's the head?"

The words rush from my lips as I stand up, still a little unsteady, and hold on to the table I've been sitting on.

"It's fine. Max. I need you to get the woman in the second row, behind where Mitchell's parents always sit. She's a brunette, wearing a white top."

Max responds cautiously, "Okaayyy. Um, Jack, I love ya, buddy, but I think what you really need right now is to rest. As much as I'm always down to help you have a little private meet and greet, now probably isn't the best time."

"It's Paige."

His eyes widen. Max knows all about Paige. He was one of the only people outside of high school who knew about my history with her, except that he knew more details than anyone else.

Max understands the significance that I am trying to convey in my tone.

"I need you to go get her and bring her to me. I have to talk to her."

"Okay, I'm on it. Behind where Mitchell's parents sit, you said?" he asks with urgency in his tone.

"Yeah."

Without another word, he hurries out the door. I begin pacing around the room, worried that she won't come, or that she's left the stadium altogether, or worst of all, that she's moved on and doesn't miss me like I miss her. How the hell have I gone almost a decade without her?

It feels like an eternity before I hear footsteps nearing the room. My heart is racing, and I can feel my breath coming heavy. My uniform feels suffocating, and I grip the front of my jersey to pull it from my neck in an effort to stop the feeling that I'm choking. Max rounds the corner, his face looking cautious and worried. I glance behind him but see only an empty hall.

"Where is she?"

He shrugs. "I'm so sorry, man. I ran to that section, but I

didn't see anyone matching her description. I even shouted her name, but it looks like she left."

My shoulders sag in defeat. Fuck. I can't believe I've lost her again.

SEVENTEEN

Paige

I splash some water on my face and try to take deep, calming breaths in a lame attempt at steadying my heart, which is still beating erratically in my chest.

The second Jack exited the field, I flew out of my seat and headed straight for the restrooms. I needed a minute to myself. Now that I've been hiding in this bathroom for the past twenty minutes, I realize that I'm even more affected by Jack than I thought I would be. I need to pull myself together. I'm not here to revert back to that silly girl who was convinced her first love would be the love of her life. I'm here to do a job. Looking in the mirror, I give myself a mini pep talk and then head back to the stands.

When I arrive at my seat, I can see that Jack has been cleared to play for the second half of the game after the medics gave him an exam during halftime. Since he's back playing, I'm assuming they didn't see any signs of a concussion, but they still seem to be keeping an eye on him as he finishes the game. Every time he comes to the sidelines, a medic is there to check in with him.

The Wolves win by a touchdown, and the stadium is

buzzing with the excitement and energy that comes with a home game victory. I follow the crowds as people leave their seats, and I make my way toward the locker rooms, where they'll be holding the postgame press conference.

I show my press credentials to the security guard and then proceed down the hall that leads to the locker room. There's a small crowd of reporters waiting outside the doors. It's standard policy that the players have fifteen to twenty minutes after the game before the press can invade.

I've always wondered how they feel about having cameras in their business while some of them are only wrapped in towels. Most tend to throw on a T-shirt in exchange for their jersey and pads and wait to shower until after the media departs. Or at least that's what our sportswriter in San Francisco used to tell me.

A media consultant ushers us all into a room right across from the locker rooms for the formal postgame interviews with the coach and one player—in this case, Jack. I tuck myself in the back, hoping I can take some time to just observe him and find my composure before I have to ask him any questions.

I thought I was prepared, but my breath catches in my throat when Jack enters behind his coach. That old pain works its way into my chest until the ache feels so real, I press a hand above my heart hoping the pressure will ease it. Cameras flash all around me as he makes his way to the table set up at the front of the room. His ass has barely touched the chair when voices start shouting questions. He throws them a panty-dropping smirk. "Alright, everyone. We've got lots of time. You'll all get a chance to ask your questions, but why don't we start one at a time, okay?"

Several reporters laugh and then one shouts out, "Jack, it looked like you were struggling at the start of the second half after that bad hit you took. Were you evaluated for a concussion?"

Jack gets a weird look on his face that I can't quite name, almost like he's disappointed. "I was evaluated and cleared, which is why I was playing the second half. I think we were playing a really strong team and they made us work for our win. I can respect that, but I wouldn't necessarily say we struggled. We won, after all," he says with a grin.

Another reporter shouts out, "Any chance you'll get back together with Bella Linn?"

My attention shoots to that reporter, then back to Jack just in time to catch his face completely shutter. Gone is the charismatic grin that he had on his face only moments ago.

I'm still stuck on the idea that he dated Bella Linn, the Victoria's Secret model. How did I miss that news?

Several more reporters start shouting similarly personal questions. I watch Jack closely and notice the subtle stiffness that seems to overcome his whole body. I'm not even sure he's breathing at this point; he looks so still. He slowly leans toward the mic.

"I will answer any questions you have about football," he emphasizes, "but my private life is private. One more question like that and this press conference will be over. Now, are there any questions about the game?"

There's a moment of silence while the reporters all try to keep from asking the invasive questions they clearly all planned to ask and attempt to come up with something focused on the game. Jack looks ready to get up and leave.

"There's talk that you'll be named the NFL's MVP of the Year. How do you feel about that?" I hear myself ask.

I can feel the weight of the stares from the other reporters, but my eyes are laser-focused on Jack. The second his gaze meets mine, his jaw drops, and his eyes go wide. We simply stare at each other for a moment, as if there's no one else around us. Finally, Jack seems to remember where he is. He takes a deep breath and then responds to my question.

"Well, that's usually an honor that goes to a player on the team that wins the Super Bowl. I'd love to make it to the Super Bowl this year, and I think we're on track to do just that."

He smirks at me, his eyes lighting up as they take me in. He subtly shakes his head like he can't believe I'm actually standing here and then answers a few more questions before wrapping up the interview. He exits, and the reporters follow, several going into the locker room to do smaller interviews with other players from the team.

I'm one of the last to exit the room and am barely out the door when a hand grips my elbow. I turn back, ready to chew someone out when my voice catches in my throat.

Jack stands before me, his eyes roaming from my head to my toes and then back up. I can't stop my own gaze from doing a similar perusal. God, why does he have to look so fucking good? His thick biceps are covered by a short-sleeved T-shirt with the Wolves logo on it. His hair is a disheveled mess, and his face is still flushed from the physical activity he just completed. I'm annoyed and frustrated with my body's complete betrayal at wishing his physical activities were more of the horizontal variety.

Ugh. I told myself during my bathroom pep talk that I wasn't going to let him affect me, and yet, here I am, my heart beating like a hummingbird's wings and a tingling starting at the apex of my thighs.

Damn him.

"I can't believe you're really standing in front of me right now," he whispers. "I almost thought I had imagined you sitting in the stands earlier."

"Nope. I'm really here." We both stare at each other for a

moment, words seemingly difficult for both of us. "It's been a long time," I whisper.

He nods. "It has. Too damn long."

I can't hide the surprise in my expression at his statement. What is that supposed to mean? How am I supposed to take that?

I cross my arms and compose my face to a more neutral expression—one I've perfected over the years when interviewing people. It has always helped me focus on the task at hand. But even with my body language screaming at him to keep a distance, my stupid heart is still pounding away at a breakneck pace in my chest.

"I don't suppose you'd be willing to do an interview for an old friend," I ask, trying to add some small playfulness to my tone that I don't feel.

His typically vibrant blue eyes dim, his brows furrow, and his mouth sags at the corners. When he speaks, his voice is not as confident as it was before. "A friend, huh? I remember you being a hell of a lot more than that."

I divert my gaze to look at our feet. "That was a long time ago. We're both very different people now."

He doesn't say anything for a long time. Finally, when I can no longer take the silence, I look back up to his face and am surprised to see misery in his gaze.

What does he have to feel miserable about? He's the one who ruined us to begin with. He's the one who came to visit me after months apart—months that were some of the hardest of my life because of how much I missed him—and then kissed me goodbye at the airport and sent me a text when he got back home saying that he couldn't do the distance anymore. He's the one who broke his promise to fight for us. He's the one who broke my fucking heart into smithereens.

Fuck him and his misery. He doesn't get to feel miserable. He made us this way.

I need to wrap this up. This is too much. I should've followed my initial instinct that I wasn't ready for this. Seeing him, being this close to him, is torture. It's bringing up too many feelings that I've long kept buried. I'll come back again and do my job once I get my head straight and my emotions under control.

"I should really get going." I take a step backward, fighting against my body's pull toward Jack.

"Wait!" He extends his arm like he wants to grab me, but then clearly thinks better of it and drops it to his side. "We should catch up. Maybe grab some dinner or something."

He looks desperate for me to say yes. I'm not sure I've ever seen this look on him before. But I can't. While my body may be trying desperately to remind me how wonderful we were together, my self-preservation instincts are fully kicking in. The reporter in me is screaming that this is the perfect opening, but that damn seventeen-year-old girl that I've hidden away is clawing her way to the surface. I know myself well enough to know I need to step back from him if I have any hope of firming up my defenses before he barrels right through them.

"I don't think that's a good idea. Take care, Jack."

I turn around, quickly exiting the hallway and ignoring his voice calling my name.

EIGHTEEN

Jack

The grooves of the brown leather offer a familiar comfort as my hand grips the football, my gaze staring at nothing while my thoughts wander to Paige. She's all I've been able to think about over the past week. The roar of the plane as we descend back into LA after our recent away game does nothing to pull me from my thoughts.

"Earth to Jack."

I turn to see Max staring at me. "Sorry, what did you say?"

"Dude, where is your head at? You've been zoning out a lot lately."

I avert my gaze, knowing my eyes will give me away. "I'm fine. Just got a lot on my mind."

"It wouldn't happen to be a beautiful brunette, would it?"

I roll my head around, trying to stretch out the tension in my neck and shoulders. "I need to figure out a way to see her again."

"You sure that's a good idea? You said she was reserved and distant with you. That doesn't exactly sound like a woman who's eager to spend time with you."

He's not wrong. The Paige who showed up to my game last week was nothing like the girl I remember. I used to know every facial expression, every smile, every thought written clear as day for me on her gorgeous face.

But the woman I encountered last week was a stranger.

I hate that.

I want to know her again, know how she's changed, how she's grown, what her interests are now.

She may have been distant with me, but that pull that always drew us together was still there. I felt it, and I refuse to believe I'm the only one.

"I can't really blame her for being guarded with me. We didn't exactly part on the best of terms." A heavy sigh escapes me as I voice the truth that I've only admitted in my most shameful thoughts. "I was a coward, and we both know it."

The small bump of the plane wheels touching the ground pulls my gaze out the window of the plane.

"I need to make things right. At the very least, she deserves to know the truth."

"And what's that?" Max asks.

Turning back to my friend, I admit to him what I'm sure he's already guessed over the years. "That she was the love of my damn life. That I regret not being strong enough to tough out the distance." Looking down at the football in my grasp, I whisper, "That I'll always love her, even if she can never forgive me."

Silence reigns between us, and it isn't until we've exited the plane and nearly made it to the car picking us up when Max speaks up.

"You said she asked for an interview."

"Yeah."

"So, what if we use that to get you another chance to clear the air with her?"

I glance at him, convinced he's not actually suggesting I give a personal interview. He must see the disbelief in my eyes because before I'm able to voice my concerns, he speaks up again.

"Hear me out. You don't have to actually give her an interview. It would be more of a carrot that you dangle for her to come to you. It would give you another chance to see her face-to-face."

"I don't know man. I think that'd piss her off even more once she realizes I'm not going to give her the interview she wants." I squeeze the bridge of my nose in an attempt to stop the pulsing that will most likely turn into a headache. "Let's drop it for now, okay? I'll figure out some way to see her again."

He hesitates, and I can tell he's not ready to drop it, but he does. "Fine. I'll drop it for now. Just don't let this distract you from the career you've worked so hard for."

We exchange a look of understanding. He's right. I wasn't at my best during our away game, but Paige was not the cause of that. Seeing her has forced me to recognize and accept responsibility for how poorly I handled everything when we were younger. I'm also trying to see it from her point of view—something I wasn't able to do back then because I was too lost in my own head.

But we're back in the same city again, and more than ever, I'm determined to make it right.

My long strides stop abruptly as soon as I walk into the empty locker room and see Max pacing.

He glances up at me, his gaze nervous and maybe a little worried. "Don't be mad."

My stomach drops as I take a few steps closer to him. "What'd you do?"

"You said you needed to see her again, so I made it happen,

even though this wasn't the way you wanted to see her." He rambles so quickly it takes a second for his words to register.

I take another step closer, my voice dropping to a dangerous rumble as I slowly ask again, "What did you do?"

Before he can answer, the door of the locker room opens behind me, and his gaze darts nervously over my shoulder. I turn around to see Paige standing there—looking more beautiful than ever—with a notebook and a small recorder clutched in one hand.

Fuck me. I glare behind me at my best friend who is on dangerously thin ice with me. He knew I didn't want to deceive her this way, and he did it anyway.

He steps closer and lowers his voice so it doesn't carry to where Paige stands near the entrance of the room.

"You told me what you needed, and I made it happen, like I always do. Don't be mad. This was the only way I could convince her to come. You sure have your work cut out for you."

"I'm sure it's even worse now that she's not going to get what she came here for," I growl under my breath, anger and frustration rolling over me in waves.

Max slaps my back and mutters, "Well, there's a limit to the miracles I can work, so now the rest is on you. Best of luck, my friend."

I try to find some composure as Max walks out the door. The last thing I need is Paige thinking I'm mad that she's here when that couldn't be further from the truth.

The click of the latch echoes into the silence of the room as Paige and I stand there staring at each other.

"Hi," I say as I grip the back of my neck with one hand and squeeze in an effort to release some of the tension in my body. "Sorry about that. I didn't know Max had reached out to you."

"You'd think your personal assistant would inform you if he was going to break your stance on exclusive interviews."

"I'm sure he would if he thought I'd actually give one."

Her already guarded gaze gets icier and her mouth forms a straight line. "So, what? You're just wasting my time then?"

I take a step forward and fight the urge to reach out to her. I can see her pulling away even more, and I have no idea how to stop it.

"No. I would like to talk to you, but I was hoping it could be off the record."

She stares at me silently, the expression on her face giving none of her feelings away. She looks down at the floor and the instant she breaks the connection, my whole body feels cold.

It's a feeling I've been all too familiar with during the last nine years without her.

"What do you say? Dinner? Tomorrow night?"

NINETEEN

Paige

I honestly don't know what to say. My head is screaming *no way in hell*, but the reporter in me is also wondering when I'm going to get this chance again. Dinner is an opportunity to get him alone, to maybe somehow convince him to share something on the record that I can use for my article. I've already turned him down once. What are the odds I'll get another chance after this? He's just given me the perfect opportunity to get what I want from him, so why am I hesitating?

Because he also makes me feel things I haven't felt since we were together, and that scares me shitless.

But at the end of the day, I have a job to do. That's all that matters.

That's all I can *let* matter.

"Fine."

His baby-blue eyes widen, and his jaw drops slightly before the corners quirk up in a smile. "Don't sound so excited about it."

I fight against my own smile because that's exactly something he would've said to me when we were in high school.

No. I cannot let him soften me. That road has only ever led me to heartbreak. Fool me once, shame on you. I won't let him fool me twice.

"It's just dinner, Jack. It doesn't change anything."

That immediately wipes the grin from his face, and I'm almost sorry for the hurt that replaces it.

"Where should I meet you?" I ask, deciding to keep things business, even if I'm feeling slightly guilty for how cold I'm being toward him.

"I'll pick you up."

God, he's persistent. I forgot about that. When he wants something, he goes after it. Always has. Maybe that's why it hurt so much when he let us go so easily.

"I think it's better if we just meet somewhere." I'm proud of myself for holding my ground, even though every moment in his presence weakens me at my core.

His eyes droop at the corners. "I hate that this is what we've become," he says, his voice whisper soft, but loud enough to reverberate around the room and hit me like a sledgehammer.

"You did this to us, Jack. Not me." My voice cracks, and I know I'm moments away from losing the carefully crafted facade making me appear completely unaffected around him.

He nods sadly. "I know I did. That doesn't make it any easier."

"I don't know what you want from me, but you're dangerously close to losing the dinner I've already agreed to." I'm bluffing. I need that dinner to get information for my article, but I also need him to stop talking about us like he's lost in memories of a time long ago when we actually meant something to each other.

Or at least when I thought we did.

He takes a step closer, his hands twitching ever so slightly at his sides. I wonder if he aches to touch me. There are times I can still feel the gentle caress of his fingers sliding through my hair and across my skin.

How have we become strangers standing across from each other with no idea how to act with one another?

Reflexively, I take a step back and watch as his gaze follows the motion. When his eyes reconnect with mine, they look so lost. Like he's wondering the same question I just asked myself.

"Fine. We'll meet there. Do you still like Italian?"

"I do."

"Okay, then I've got just the place. I'll text you the address and meet you there at seven."

"Max can give you my number. I'll see you then," I say, my voice shockingly composed, even though my insides feel like a knotted mess. I quickly spin around and exit the way I came, my earlier escort long gone. That's fine. The time alone gives me time to pull myself together and get my head on straight.

If ten minutes in a room with him left me this much of a wreck, how the hell am I supposed to get through an entire dinner?

My fist raps gently against the door to make my presence known. "You wanted to see me?"

Vince sits regally at his desk, his shoulders back and head held high like he has all the confidence in the world. I wish I felt the same, but there's been a knot growing in my stomach since the moment Vince forced this assignment on me.

"Any luck with Fuller?"

As if a fist is squeezing that knot, my stomach clenches. I debate for a moment whether I should tell him the truth or not.

Going with honesty, I share, "We're having dinner tonight actually."

A wicked gleam fills his eyes, and a grin that's reminiscent of the Grinch spreads across his face. "Excellent. Glad to hear you're moving things along. I'd love to get an update afterward."

That knot in my stomach grows as I force the words from my lips. "Sure thing."

A copy editor rushes into the room. "I've got those changes you wanted to see."

"I'll leave you to deal with that," I say, thankful for the excuse to escape without having to discuss my dinner with Jack any further. Something about sharing details with Vince feels slimy, even though it's my job.

The second I turn around from shutting Vince's door, my body slams into someone, and a high-pitched squeal escapes from the poor woman's throat before she stumbles backward, dropping all the papers she was carrying.

"Oh God, I'm so sorry," I say as I bend down to help her pick up the papers now scattered on the floor between us.

"It's totally fine." Her melodic voice should be soothing, but there's something slightly fake about it.

"No, it isn't. I should've been paying more attention. Are you okay?" I ask, finally looking up to see the young woman I just bumped into. Her dark brown hair is silky smooth and falls straight around her shoulders. Her vividly bright blue eyes seem almost shocking against her creamy skin and cherry red lipstick. Her eyes brighten when they meet mine.

"You're Paige O'Malley, right?"

"Yeah. How'd you know?"

She rolls her eyes in an exaggerated way that makes me think of one of the lead characters in *Clueless*. "The staff meeting last week. Vince pointed you out."

"Oh, right," I say, totally having forgotten about last week's brief staff meeting with all the other Jack craziness that has suddenly consumed my life. I grab the last paper and we both rise together.

"That's quite the stack you've got there." I gesture to the cluttered papers piled sloppily in her hands.

She looks down at them and then smiles ruefully. "Research." She tilts her head to Vince's door and gets a slight glint in her eyes. "Gotta prove to the boss that I'm worth keeping around. You know how it goes."

I nod in understanding, remembering all too well the many nights I stayed behind long after everyone else had gone home just to prove my worth. I'd almost trade going back to those days in order to avoid having to be in a room with Jack again.

"Well, best of luck with that."

"Thanks," she says in her bubbly voice, before she continues walking the direction she was headed. She's only taken a few steps before I call out, "Hey, wait a sec."

She turns around, her perfectly sculpted brow arching ever so slightly. "Yeah?"

"I never got your name. Seems only fair since you know mine."

"It's Alicia. Alicia Fitzgerald."

I offer her a warm smile and extend my hand. "It's a pleasure to meet you, Alicia."

She takes my hand and offers me a smile of her own, this one not quite matching the bright personality she's carried throughout our whole exchange.

"The pleasure's all mine."

TWENTY

Jack

The reflection staring back at me as I put on my jacket doesn't match the usual confident jock I've become so used to. Instead, I'm feeling the same rush of nerves I felt when I first realized my feelings for Paige had changed from friendship to so much more. Back when I thought I'd found the person I would be with for the rest of my life.

I'd give anything to go back to that boy and tell him not to let her go.

Instead, I stare at my reflection for a minute longer, preparing for the night ahead. There's a desperation clawing underneath my skin telling me this might be my only shot to get Paige to spend more time with me. With one last deep breath, I attempt to shake off the unfamiliar nerves, and head to the restaurant where we agreed to meet.

The drive is quick, and I'm grateful because I'm dangerously distracted by all the different scenarios playing out in my mind. The most unrealistic one—where Paige tells me she still loves me—is the one I want the most, but I know that's beyond wishful thinking at this point. She's made it perfectly clear I'm not high on her list of favorite people. And I can't even be mad about it because I put myself in this position.

The restaurant is dimly lit with most of the light coming from the simple and elegant fixtures—reminding me of a Hershey's kiss because of their shape—hanging above each table. I look around the lobby, and then check my watch when I don't see Paige. I hope she didn't get lost.

The thought barely crosses my mind before the door opens and she walks in, looking like a vision in a gorgeous black dress that hugs her delicate curves and stops midthigh. My mouth goes dry as my gaze falls down her body, taking in her long, tanned, and toned legs. My heart pounds furiously inside my chest and I feel almost breathless. How does Paige always have this ability to make me completely speechless? Since we were sixteen, she's had this effect on me. Even when other women were around, my attention never strayed from her.

God, I'm a fucking idiot for letting her go.

"Sorry I'm late. Traffic," she says with an almost sheepish smile.

"No worries. I just got here myself." I want to tell her how beautiful she looks, but her hands are fidgeting with her clutch, and her eyes keep darting around the room like she's nervous and doesn't want to make eye contact with me. My stomach drops. We were never like this before, and I hate that this is what we've become. We are two strangers who don't know how to act around each other.

"Mr. Fuller, your table is ready," the hostess interrupts our awkward standoff. If there were other patrons waiting in the lobby, I'm sure they would probably think we were on the most uncomfortable first date in the history of the world.

I gesture for Paige to go ahead of me. "After you."

She gives me a small smile that doesn't quite reach her eyes, mutters a thanks, and then follows the hostess. We meander through the tables in the front to a more secluded booth in the back. Maybe that's a good thing. No one to witness me crash and burn as I try to win over the only woman I've ever loved.

"Thanks," Paige mutters as the hostess sets the menus in front of us once we are seated. I'm kicking myself for not thinking to pull back her chair for her. Or maybe that would've been too much. Fuck. I have no idea how to act around Paige anymore.

Silence reigns at the table until the waitress comes over, introducing herself and bringing us glasses of water. I'd originally planned not to have any alcohol during this dinner because I wanted to be completely clearheaded during our conversation, but when Paige orders a glass of wine, I quickly jump on the alcohol bandwagon and order a whiskey on the rocks.

Paige takes a tentative sip of her water while her gaze wanders around the room, still avoiding eye contact with me, I notice.

"So," I say, clearing my throat, and trying to figure out how to break the ice. "How've you been?"

She quirks a brow and her lips tilt up ever so slightly at the corners. "Really? That's how you want to start the conversation? Is that the new 'So, how about this weather'?" Her tone is more playful than I've heard from her since first seeing her at my game.

Leaning my elbows on the table, I respond, "Well, I'd ask something else if I thought you'd answer."

"And what would that be?"

All pretense washes away. "Did you ever think about us?" I regret being so direct the second the words leave my mouth because her playful demeanor instantly vanishes, and in its place is the reserved woman she's been.

"You're right. I'm not going to answer that."

I sit back in my chair, deflated like a balloon and trying to figure out how to get back what we had just a minute ago.

Why can't I ever get things right with her?

The waitress returns, and we place our orders. I watch Paige carefully, but she's back to avoiding my gaze at all costs. I'm almost tempted to offer her one question on the record, but everything inside me revolts at the idea.

"I'm sorry." The words leave my mouth before I even process what I've said. Her gaze snaps to mine, but she doesn't say anything. "I shouldn't have asked that. It's just..." I trail off, not really knowing what to say.

I know what I *want* to say, but I don't know if it's worth her shutting down even more than she already is. Then again, what if this is my only chance to really be honest with her?

"It's just what?" she asks, her voice soft and cautious.

I meet her gaze, her chocolate-brown eyes mesmerizing me the way they always have. "I missed the hell out of you."

"Jack—"

"No, I need to get this out. I've spent nine years being silent, and I've regretted every single second. I loved you, Paige. You were the love of my damn life and I let you go because I was scared. Every day felt like a fucking eternity without you, and the idea of going through that for another year—possibly longer since we hadn't talked college plans at that point—made me feel like I was dying." I take a breath, my chest aching as I open old wounds that never healed properly. "I had no idea letting you go would feel so much worse. By the time I fully realized what a colossal mistake I'd made, too much time had passed. I didn't know how to fix it. I didn't know what to say to you."

"Anything," she says, her glassy eyes the only hint that this is affecting her as much as it is me. "You could've said anything, Jack. But you didn't. You promised you'd fight for us. Before I moved, you swore you'd fight, and you didn't. You didn't." Her voice cracks along with her carefully composed exterior, and I recognize all the hurt that she's been carrying because it matches my own.

"I know," I say, my voice barely a whisper as I fight against the lump of emotion in my throat. "No amount of words will be enough to convey how sorry I am, Paige. But if this is the only chance I ever get to tell you how I really feel, I'm gonna take it."

With a deep breath for courage, I confess, "I've never stopped loving you."

"You don't even know me anymore."

My blood heats, and I hate that she's partially right, but only partially. "I might not know your interests now or what you've done for the past nine years, but I still know you. I know who you are deep down. I know what shaped you growing up. That doesn't just vanish. That's part of who you are. Hell, it's part of who I am. I wouldn't be half the man I am today if it weren't for you, Paige—for having you in my life as my best friend growing up and loving you as hard as I always have. My fuckup with us doesn't change any of that."

"How can you possibly say that? It changed everything." I swear I see fire spark in her eyes, but I'll take this over the neutral version she was giving me before.

"It changed nothing when it comes to how I feel about you. That's never changed, Paige. Never. It's always been you. It'll always *be* you."

Her eyes widen, and her jaw goes slack before she starts shaking her head back and forth. "It's too late," she whispers. "I can't do this. Tonight was a mistake."

Nine years ago, I thought my heart shattered into a million irreparable pieces when I made the worst mistake of my life. But Paige proves there's still more to break as she walks swiftly out of the restaurant, crushing the rest of my heart to smithereens.

TWENTY-ONE

Paige

I stare at the white ceiling above my bed, my body aching as if I've gone forty rounds with The Rock. But it's just my stupid, conflicted heart that's battering the rest of my body.

Jack's words have been in a never-ending loop in my head since our almost dinner last night. No matter what I do to try to think of something else—including the desperate measure of playing "It's a Small World" on repeat—nothing works.

I can't stop seeing the tortured and heartbroken look on his handsome face or hearing the pain in his words. The torment I felt all those months immediately after he broke my heart was written all over his face. For the first time in nine years, I'm realizing that I wasn't alone in my heartbreak. He was right there with me—physically across the country, but emotionally feeling everything I was feeling.

I want desperately to still be angry at him. To still be filled with furious rage at how easily he let us go.

But I can't.

Not after last night.

Because if there's anything that became abundantly clear

last night, it's that nothing about our breakup was easy on him. Not a damn thing.

So where the hell does that leave us?

I don't have an answer as my alarm goes off and I blink my bleary eyes and roll out of bed. On autopilot, I get ready for work, going through my morning routine like a mindless robot while that question joins the barrage of Jack's words in my head. I get to work and can barely remember how I got there. It's not until I sit down at my desk and stare at my blank screen that I recall I'm supposed to be writing an exclusive about Jack.

Guilt curls like an anchor in my stomach, feeling heavy and weighing me down. I close my eyes, desperate to escape this feeling, but all I can see are Jack's hauntingly beautiful blue eyes.

"O'Malley!" Vince's booming voice shouts, and I open my eyes and turn in my chair to see him standing outside his office door. "My office."

I stand up on shaky legs and try to find whatever composure I can as I make my way to his office.

"You wanted to see me?"

"How'd the dinner go? Were you able to get anything good?" Vince's eyes are bright with excitement, and I swear he's salivating at the idea that I got the exclusive he's desperate for.

The exclusive that now feels more impossible than ever. And not because I don't want to spend time with Jack but because the more his words penetrate the armor I've built up over the years, the more I *do* want to spend time with him. To see if he's right that deep down we still know each other. That maybe we can heal our old hurts.

Together.

"Uh, he actually had to cancel." It's the only excuse I can think of that might buy me some time to figure out what the hell I'm going to do.

Vince's eyes turn to slits. "He canceled?" he asks, disbe-lievingly.

"Yep."

He stares at me, like he can taste the lie in the air and wants to call my bluff. Instead, he says, "Have you rescheduled?"

"Um, not yet."

"What are you waiting for?" His excited demeanor has turned shockingly hard in a short amount of time.

I hesitate, worried I'm digging myself into a lie that I can't get out of—one of the reasons I hate lying to begin with. "He needed to check his schedule."

Vince stares at me. "Fine. But don't put it off too long. We need that article, Paige."

"I understand. I'll follow up with him tonight."

"You do that," he says, his shrewd eyes making my skin itch from fear that he saw right through me.

Without another word, I escape his office and head back to my cubicle. I have no idea what I'm going to do, but if that exchange with Vince was any indication, I need to figure it out quick.

TWENTY-TWO

Jack

Are you free tomorrow?

I stare at the text for a minute in sheer disbelief. I was sure that after Paige walked out of our dinner yesterday, I'd never see her again.

I rack my brain to remember what I have planned for tomorrow, but nothing pressing comes to mind. I text Max and ask him to rearrange my schedule tomorrow so it's clear and then I text Paige back.

Me: I'm free.

My mind goes completely blank, and my thumbs hover uselessly over my phone's keyboard as I try to figure out what else to say. I feel like I'm walking in a minefield and the wrong thing might cause an explosion to go off, causing the whole conversation to end as abruptly as it started.

Did you want to get together? I add before pressing send and hoping that was the right thing.

I swear I'm not usually so unsure when it comes to women, but then again, Paige is no ordinary woman. She's *the* woman.

Paige: Yeah, I'd like that.

Then a second later another text comes through from her that has my heart racing.

Paige: *I've been thinking a lot about what you said.*

And? I type out as fast as I can.

Paige: *I think we owe it to ourselves to talk and clear the air.*

That's not a confession of undying love, but it's not a rejection either. It's an opening, a chance to finally deal with all our baggage and maybe start a new future.

God, I'd give anything for her to be open to having a future together.

I think back on our conversation yesterday and then come up with a plan. After some quick research and a few phone calls to confirm I can make it happen, I text her back.

Me: *Do you trust me?*

I know it's a big ask, but for my plans to go off without her getting spooked, I need her trust.

Paige: *I don't know.*

My heart sinks at her response, but I don't get to respond before another one quickly follows.

Paige: *I want to.*

That's a start.

Me: *I'll take it.*

I text her an address which will take her to my favorite hiking trail in Topanga State Park and tell her what to wear. I want her to be comfortable but also prepared without spoiling the surprise. And as much as I wish she'd ride with me, I don't want to push her too far out of her comfort zone. I suspect driving herself will make her feel more comfortable.

The next day, I'm a ball of nerves as I drive to Topanga Mountain. I've never felt this level of nerves before—not even when I started for my first NFL game, when we were playing the top team in the league and a quarterback I had always aspired to be like.

When I arrive, Paige is already in the lot sitting in her car, but it doesn't appear that anyone else is here yet today. I hope it stays quiet. This trail is one of my favorites because it's not usually as busy as the more well-known ones, which means less chance of someone recognizing me and interrupting my time with Paige.

Getting out of my car, I grab my backpack filled with snacks and water and make my way over to Paige, who's now standing outside her car, her arms wrapped around her while her gaze is staring off into the distance, roving over the beautiful, serene view.

My whole body comes to life in a way it hasn't in years. Not since her. And the ache to hold her close is so strong, but I know I haven't earned that privilege.

Yet.

"Hey," I say softly, not wanting to disturb the quiet serenity surrounding us. Her gaze turns from the view to me.

"Hey," she says.

"Thanks for reaching out. I'm glad you wanted to get together again."

She stares at me for a moment, her expression unreadable, before she nibbles on her lip. The movement sends me back ten years to when she'd do that whenever she was nervous.

"I'm nervous too," I say, hoping I can put her at ease. Hell, it's the truth. I have no idea what will come after today.

She offers a small smile. "Am I that obvious?"

I point to my own lip. "You're chewing on your lip. You always used to do that when you were nervous."

Her smile fades, but the look in her eyes doesn't seem sad. Maybe wary, or unsure.

"I guess maybe there are some things you still know about me," she says, her voice barely a whisper.

"I'd like to know it all."

She continues to stare at me, her gaze burrowing into my soul until my entire body feels warm just from being around her. What I would give to experience this for the rest of my life.

"Maybe we should start with college."

"Sure." I hesitate, knowing I need to say it but wishing I didn't. "All of this is off the record."

Her wary gaze turns sad before she nods her head. I can't tell if she's sad because she was hoping to get a story or because I had to say it at all.

We start our hike and spend the first mile or so talking about our college years. She tells me about her best friend, Gina, and the adventures they got into, while I tell her all about Max and my college days, although they were mostly filled with football. By the time we stop for some water and a snack, I'm both dreading and eager to talk about the one topic that's been hanging over our heads for nearly ten years.

As we sit in silence, looking out over the view and sipping from our water bottles, I contemplate how to start.

But she beats me to it. "We should probably talk about what happened with us."

I glance at her, noting she doesn't move her gaze away from the view. Is she as afraid of this conversation as I am?

"Yeah, we probably should."

"I'm not even sure where to start," she admits with a weak laugh.

"Ask me anything."

She turns to me then, her gaze penetrating. "Why didn't you fight for us?"

She might as well have punched me in the heart for the effect her words have on me.

I look down at my hands, shame and memories from those first few days after breaking up with her washing over me. "I wish I had a good answer, but I don't. Each day apart felt like an eternity, which sounds comical now that I've spent nine years regretting it. A year, maybe a few more due to college, was really nothing, but at the time..." I look up at the view, not having the guts to face her but wanting her to know the truth. "At the time, everything felt like it was falling apart without you there. My grades slipped, I kept making mistakes on the field, to the point Coach threatened to bench me until I could get my head on straight. And you were so far away. Our conversations seemed to get more strained and superficial with each day that passed, and I didn't know what to do."

My gaze moves to hers, because I need her to know this next part with all the sincerity I can convey. "I never meant to end it the way I did. I planned to do it in person. But then I saw you, and everything felt amazing again. We had a perfect week together, and it wasn't until that morning when you took me to the airport that I realized my chance to do it was quickly evaporating. Time was moving too fast, and you seemed so happy. The truth is I didn't want to see you hate me. I didn't want to see all that love in your eyes disappear the moment I broke your heart. So I walked away and took the coward's way out. And I've regretted it every day since."

"Breaking up with me that way?"

"Breaking up with you at all."

She inhales sharply, and her eyes brim with tears as her gaze locks on mine. I hold my breath, waiting, convinced more than ever that this woman holds my heart in the palm of her hands, and at any moment she could crush it.

TWENTY-THREE

Paige

My breath is stuck in my lungs as I stare at the one man who's always had my heart—even when I didn't want him to. There's no doubt about the sincerity of his words. His eyes have always given him away, and there's nothing but honesty there.

And love.

It took me a while to recognize it after all these years, but it's been there from the first moment we saw each other again.

"Jack..." I don't know what to say. So many emotions are clamoring to the surface right now. It's overwhelming feeling everything that I've kept buried for so long. I'm still hurt, but I understand better now. So, where does that leave us?

He doesn't speak. He just watches me with his emotions written all over his face.

"Jack, I...I don't know where to go from here."

He reaches out and grabs my hand, the connection sending a flare of warmth and familiarity through my body. God, it feels good to hold his hand again. Mine always fit so perfectly in his, his large warm fingers wrapping securely around my own.

"Give me another chance." His eyes plead with me, but not in a desperate way that would normally be a turnoff. Instead, it's hopeful, almost like he's convinced if I give him another chance, our whole future could be different.

Maybe it could.

But can I take that risk?

"Okay," I say, my voice a breathless whisper.

His bright baby-blue eyes light up, and his thumb moves to brush across the apple of my cheek. I can't stop the sharp inhale of breath, even if I wanted to. Nor can I deny that his touch sends warmth pulsing straight to my core. All of my defenses are screaming at me to hit the brakes, but for once I ignore them and lean in ever so slightly until Jack and I are only a breath apart.

"Paige," he says reverently. "Am I dreaming?"

"No."

"Thank fuck," he exhales and then his lips are on mine, and I'm completely lost to the sensation of his lips caressing mine with the same ease that was always there. His hand slides into my hair as his tongue licks across the seam of my lips. On a soft gasp, I open and welcome his tongue with my own.

My entire body feels like it's engulfed in flames, the heat incinerating any reservations I had about giving him another chance. He owns me with a kiss. I'm increasingly thankful that we were already sitting down because this is definitely a kiss that makes you weak in the knees. He pulls away before I'm ready to let him go, but I don't protest because my brain is now a scrambled mess.

His thumb grazes my cheek, and his eyes shine with joy. "That was better than I remember."

I nod, still incapable of forming sentences.

He stares at me for a moment longer, almost like he can't believe I'm real. That we're really doing this. I almost can't believe it either.

But then, Jack Fuller's always been my weak spot.

It's not until we're almost back to our cars that my head

clears enough for a realization to burst through my happy bubble.

How the hell am I going to get out of Vince's assignment now?

Jack's schedule has kept him busy for the last week, which I thought would be a problem for our newly rekindled relationship, but it hasn't been an issue. He's called me every night and asked about my day. It's been easy to fall back into our old comfort with each other. I thought there would be some awkwardness, but there hasn't been any. The only thing that's been hard is not being able to tell him about the article that I'm supposed to be writing on him.

At the thought of my career, my stomach dips. Vince has been hounding me more and more about the article and if there have been any new developments. It'd be easier to hold off a rabid dog than my editor. As I drove to the stadium tonight, I told myself to finally tell Jack the truth, but every time I even consider it, my stomach clenches with dread. I feel like we're still on shaky ground and we've barely even been together.

I don't want to risk it.

For the first time ever, I'm putting a man before my career, and that's terrifying in its own right.

The game starts, and I watch Jack play incredibly through the night. I also don't miss that he takes the opportunity to look at me whenever he's on the sidelines. Each time our eyes meet, a smile lights his face, and it takes my breath away.

How did I stay away from him for so long?

It seemed so easy to be away from him before, simply because pride and necessity demanded it. But being this close to him, I am drawn to him more than ever.

I always longed for him, but I had an easier time convincing myself that I was doing the right thing by not trying to contact him before, by burying all those feelings until I convinced myself they didn't exist. Now, all those reasons are flying right out the window.

I keep telling myself that I need to guard my heart—feeling this strongly for him is dangerous, especially with how things ended last time. Not to mention that so much time has passed.

But we still seem like two magnets, always drawn together.

Max comes at the end of the game to take me back to meet Jack. The locker room is cleared out except for Jack, who looks more handsome than ever in a pair of well-fitted jeans and a T-shirt that shows off his deliciously sculpted arms. His dark brown hair is short on the sides and longer on top, and my fingers itch to run through it. His blue eyes scan my body, and my breath stalls in my chest as I do the same to him.

Damn, Jack has filled out so much. His body is male perfection, and I find my body responding to him in the same ways it always has—that rapid staccato of my heart, the heating of my cheeks as dirty thoughts spin wildly in my mind, and the pulse between my thighs reminding me how good he always made me feel when we were together.

A bright smile breaks across his face when he catches me checking him out, and I can feel my cheeks heating from being caught.

"Hey," he says softly as he moves toward me and gives me a light kiss on the cheek. He's so tender it makes my heart melt.

"Hey."

"You ready to go?"

"What about my car? Should I follow you?"

"We can come back for it. I'd rather talk to you on the way, if that's okay with you."

"Sure." As soon as the reply leaves my mouth, I feel his

hand at the small of my back as he guides me out to the team parking lot.

I shouldn't be surprised to see that he has more than one car, the sleek, black Range Rover a different vehicle than the truck he drove to our hike.

"Impressive car. You know, all these years I kept picturing you in your BMW from high school."

"You kept picturing me?" he asks with what sounds like a tinge of hope in his voice.

I belatedly realize that I've exposed more than I meant to with that statement. We've talked about our breakup and some of the years that followed, but never much more about how we felt about the other after our breakup. Instead of playing it off I decide to be honest with him.

"Yeah. I've followed your career here and there. I watched you during the draft. I don't think I've ever seen your parents so proud of you, as they should be. You got everything you ever wanted."

"Not everything," he whispers.

My smile drops at the serious expression on his face, and it feels as if all the air in the car evaporates. I know now exactly what he's referring to. It's impossible not to after his confession on our hike last week. This whole time he's wanted me. I take a shaky breath and try to find some composure. There are still moments where all of this feels like some parallel universe. Although, I guess in a parallel universe Jack and I never would've broken up in the first place.

He clears his throat. "I still have the BMW. It's in my garage with a couple of other cars I own."

"How many cars do you have? I didn't expect you to become a car collector. Following Leno's footsteps?" I tease, trying to get back to that ease we had before.

His smile returns as he lets out a chuckle. "Something like

that. I don't know how it happened, really. I had the BMW, then bought a Mercedes with my first signing bonus, then I got a kick-ass deal on a Ferrari, which of course, I couldn't pass up."

"Of course," I confirm.

"Eventually, I decided I wanted something a little larger with more space, so I got this bad boy." He affectionately rubs the dashboard. "I also have the Ford Raptor for whenever I need to transport any kind of loads. It came in handy when I moved into my house."

"So now you have five cars?"

"Actually, I have six. I got a Subaru after I did some promotional work for a local dealership." He glances over at me. "What about you? Anything you unintentionally collect?"

I think about it for all of five seconds. "Coffee mugs. It started in college. I unintentionally took one from the student union building once after eating breakfast, and by the time I graduated, I had this insane collection that I'd either bought or been gifted. It seemed whenever I was in souvenir shops or something, I'd buy a cute mug. My friends found out about it and started adding to my collection. Now, I have like fifty. I don't have the heart to part with any of them, even though I only use a few over and over again. But they each carry a memory, so I don't want to get rid of any."

"Coffee mugs fit with the whole journalist thing."

"Yeah, I suppose they do."

"You're not the only one who's been keeping track, you know? I've followed your career."

Shock floods my face. He's been keeping tabs on me?

He continues, "I've probably read a majority of the articles you've published. If it was online, I read it. You're really good." He furtively glances in my direction, a blush forming on his cheeks. I find it endearing, and my shock turns to relief knowing that he looked into me as much as I looked into him.

"I especially liked when you covered that football game at San Francisco University two years ago. It reminded me of when you'd talk about my games with me," he says.

I shake my head in disbelief. "I can't believe you remember an article from so long ago."

"I remember a lot of things from further back than that." The look he gives me is heated with desire, and I can feel the goosebumps spread across my suddenly flushed skin. Before I can respond, he parks in front of a tiny restaurant called Olive Oil. The ambiance in the restaurant is modern romance with votive candles in the center of each table and soft overhead lighting, but the rest is all modern décor that is surprisingly comfortable.

We're seated at a table tucked in the back corner. Jack's fame comes with certain perks since our table offers the perfect amount of privacy to ensure eager fans won't interrupt us while we eat.

Our waitress hands us menus and walks away to get us some waters and our beverages—whiskey for Jack, red wine for me. We both pick up our menus to look at the selection, but my gaze wanders up and over to glance at Jack. I can see the definition of his pecs through his snug shirt.

God, seriously, why does he have to be so sexy?

"I'm gonna need you to stop looking at me like that."

My eyes shoot up to his face, and it's clear he's fighting a smirk.

My cheeks heat as I blush. Damn, he caught me ogling him. "Sorry," I mumble and move my gaze back to my menu.

"Paige."

"Hmm?" I murmur, my eyes glued to my paper in front of me, although I have no idea what I'm actually reading right now because I'm still picturing Jack's toned chest and the heated desire I saw in his eyes.

"Paige. Look at me," he demands.

I sigh and then look up. The second our eyes meet, it's like the temperature in the restaurant skyrockets. When did it become a hundred degrees in here?

"You have nothing to be embarrassed about."

Damn, he caught the blush. I was hoping the restaurant lighting would hide it.

"But if you keep looking at me like you are now, all I'm going to want to eat is you."

My jaw drops at the implication.

Oh, yes, please, my body begs.

Have I mentioned it's been a long time since I've had sex? Jack sitting there looking fucking drool-worthy is any sane woman's fantasy. I'd be crazy not to respond to his boldness.

I clear my throat, trying to cover up my ridiculous reaction to him. When he smiles knowingly—the cocky bastard— I realize I am not playing this smooth and sophisticated at all. I shake my head at him, and he laughs, picking up his menu and continuing to peruse the options.

The intensity between us grows as we look over our menus, glancing at each other every so often. By the time the waitress has taken our order, the air feels thick from the tension flowing between us.

Jack takes a smooth sip of his whiskey on the rocks and then leans forward, his elbows resting on the table. "So, how long have you been in LA?"

This is good. A topic that isn't sex-related. "Just a couple of weeks actually. I recently got hired at the *LA Chronicle,* which you already know."

He shrugs unapologetically. I wasn't even surprised that he found out where I worked after that first press conference. His fame comes with connections, one of those being the ability to find information. But it just confirms that he could've found me sooner if he really wanted to. That thought sedates the desire pumping through my blood. I break eye contact and shift uncomfortably in my seat.

Jack must be able to tell that something has changed because he gives me a curious look that quickly morphs to determination. "What made you want to be a journalist?"

"I took a class in high school and really enjoyed it."

His brow furrows. "I don't remember that."

I shift again in my chair. "It was after we broke up."

"Oh." He drops his gaze to the table, and I'd pay a million dollars to know what he's thinking right now. When he lifts his eyes, the resolve in them pierces me straight in the heart.

"I'm determined to make this work, Paige. I know there are going to be things that come up that make us both uncomfortable. I know our breakup is still a sore spot for you just like it is for me, but I also don't want our past to hold us back. There's still something between us. I know you can feel it."

I take a sip of my wine to clear my throat before responding. "You're right."

"I've made mistakes, but I'm trying to fix them. So ask whatever you want."

I know he's opening the door for me to ask about our relationship but I'm not quite ready for that yet. "Why do you refuse to give personal interviews to the press?"

He sits back in his chair, disappointment coating his features. "Are you asking as a reporter or as my date?"

"Is there a difference?"

"You know there is."

He's right, I do. If I'm asking as a reporter, then that means this won't go anywhere, and whatever we've just restarted will come to an abrupt end. I'll have made my intentions clear. If I'm asking as his date, then it means I'm open to us really having a second chance to make things work. It means my job is no longer the priority.

Am I asking as a reporter or his date?

My job was the last thing on my mind as I got ready to see him tonight. I just wanted to see him after a week apart. Whether he knows it or not, I made my choice the moment I kissed him.

He's watching me cautiously, nerves written clearly on his face. "Paige?"

"I'm here as your date," I whisper, my eyes pleading with him. *Don't make me regret this.*

His shoulders sag in relief, and he nods his head once before replying to my earlier question. "I was never a huge fan of media digging into my personal life. Then I got burned by my girlfriend junior year of college, and that pretty much solidified my resolve to never give the media anything unless it's related to football."

I rack my brain for what he could be referring to with his ex. I did massive research on him before going to that first game. I never found anything from his college days.

"What happened with your girlfriend?"

He takes another sip of his whiskey. "I caught her fucking my teammate the night before our championship game in the Lemon Cup."

I inhale sharply. I definitely would've remembered a story like that. "I never saw or heard anything about that." I don't tell him that I'm referring to my recent research. I remember seeing posts on social media of him with some blonde his junior year of college. I didn't look into him for over a year after that. When I did finally read his social media accounts again, I didn't see anything about a cheating scandal.

"It was big news for about three months, but then other scandals happened, and my dad helped bury anything that was still out there." He shrugs like it's no big deal, but I can tell that experience affected him immensely. Jack's always been insanely loyal. I can't imagine how much that hurt to have her cheat on him.

"I'm so sorry you went through that. Nobody deserves to be cheated on."

He brushes off my sympathy. "It sucked, but honestly, we should've broken up months before. We weren't right for each other."

I nod my head. I can relate to that.

"How about you?" he asks.

"How about me, what?"

"Any exes who screwed you over?"

I give him a hard look, and his face blanches as he registers the words that just came out of his mouth.

"Uh, I mean, besides me, I guess," he mumbles awkwardly.

"I haven't had the best of luck with the men I've dated," I respond honestly.

"Me either," he says. "But I know the reason why none of my relationships ever worked."

I look at him curiously. "Why?"

His penetrating gaze is fierce as he responds heavily, "None of them were you."

My breathing becomes shallow as I watch his face, searching for any clue that he might be joking, but his expression holds nothing but open honesty.

The waitress breaks the spell when she shows up with our food. The rest of the meal is spent talking about lighter topics. I'm stuffed by the time I finish my meal, but more than that, my heart feels fuller than it has in a very long time.

By the time he drops me off at my car, the only thing holding me back from fully embracing the chemistry that zings between us is the fact that I still have this article assignment hanging over my head. I don't want to tell Jack about how hard my editor is pushing me to write a piece on him. Honestly, I don't want to tell him about the article at all. We're getting along, but it still feels fragile. I can't ruin this second chance.

I get out of his SUV, preparing myself to say goodbye, even though I really wish the night didn't have to end. Despite the moments of awkwardness and the crazy sexual tension, it felt really good to just be with him again.

It felt like coming home.

He meets me at my door and cups my cheek with his large, calloused palm, the warmth from his hand feeling like heaven. He leans down to kiss me, but this isn't a chaste kiss like I was expecting. The moment our lips meet, passion explodes within me. I grip his hair, moan into his mouth, and give in to everything I'm feeling. All the longing, the desire, the confusion, and the fear that he'll break my heart again. I let it all go in that kiss, and he takes it all, his own mouth eagerly molding with mine. I don't know how long we stand there passionately kissing before he reluctantly pulls his lips from mine.

"God, Paige, you have no idea what you do to me," he whispers as he leans his forehead against mine.

"Ditto," I whisper back.

He smiles before placing one more quick kiss on my lips and then opening my car door for me. I wave to Jack as I pull away from him, my heart beating profusely and my mind made up. I need to talk to Vince. For the first time ever, I'm putting my career second.

When I get home and see that Jack has already texted me asking when he can see me next, I know I'm making the right decision.

Now I just need to talk to Vince.

TWENTY-FOUR

Jack

I smile at the message emblazoned on my phone screen.

Paige: I can't wait to see you.

My head rests on my seat as the plane ascends, and the noise around me fades while thoughts of Paige swarm my mind. I can still hear her laugh from our phone call last night ringing in my ears. There has never been a sweeter sound in the world.

I'll admit I was hard as a rock by the time we got off the phone and came embarrassingly fast when I stroked myself thinking about Paige.

I glance out the window, eager for this flight to be over already. It's only been a week since I've seen Paige, but even after nearly a decade of separation, a week feels like too much. I'm done being away from her.

Although they aren't my favorite, away games never felt like torture before; I always prefer a home-field advantage. But being away from Paige for seven whole days after reconnecting with her feels like pure torment. Yet, despite the distance, it was the least alone I had felt in years. Just hearing her voice on the other end of the phone every night was like a soothing balm.

The icing on the cake, though, was rediscovering that our

connection is as strong as ever. It was like the last nine years never really happened. Talking with her has been as easy as it was when we were kids. I swear I've laughed more this past week than I have since Paige and I dated.

The hardest part has been the relentless boners. Pun intended. I swear just hearing her voice makes me rock hard. I'm certain that I've developed new callouses on my hand from the number of times I've had to jack off this week. I don't remember any woman ever provoking this kind of response from me.

Max disrupts my thoughts with a bump to my elbow. "I'm guessing that smirk on your face has to do with the lovely Paige."

I turn toward him to see my grin reflected on his face. "It does."

"Dude, you know I love you like you were my own brother, but I never realized what an asshole you were until Paige came back into the picture. I don't know how she did it, but it's like she's smoothed out all your rough spots. You've been in a ridiculously good mood. If I didn't know any better, I'd say you'd been getting laid regularly."

I ignore his getting laid comment since he knows I've stayed in my room instead of partying with the team each night. My only company this week has been my hand.

"I wasn't that big of an asshole before."

"No, you weren't terrible, but now that I've seen the difference, it's pretty noticeable."

I shrug. "Nothing's really happened with Paige yet. We've only had the hike and then that one dinner date."

"And you talk every night," he points out with another grin on his face. "You want something to happen, right?"

I can't stop the you're-fucking-joking-right face from emerging. "Of course, I want something to happen. It's Paige. She's the woman I've compared all others to. Hell, my refusal to let go of Paige is what drove Kallie to cheat; and I didn't even care when she left.

"Paige is what I've been missing all this time. Leaving her at that airport in Chicago and then breaking up with her all those years ago has always been my biggest regret. I want nothing more than to make something happen with Paige, preferably something permanent."

He sits up and his grin drops. "Woah, are you serious? I don't think I've ever heard you mention anything remotely related to marriage before. Are you sure you want to go there that quickly? I mean, you guys just reconnected."

"I'm as serious as a heart attack. She's the one. I can feel it with every fiber of my being. She's what I've been missing. She's who I need in my life. Everything feels right when I'm with her."

I have no doubt if Paige hadn't moved, we'd probably already be married with a couple of kids. Max stares at me, his mouth slightly agape in shock. He's right; I've never talked about anyone like this. But I've also never loved anyone the way I love Paige.

"Okay..." He hesitates and looks at me cautiously. "What about the fact that she's a journalist? Aren't you worried that she could write something about you?"

I glance out the window at the endless white clouds. I've thought a lot about that since she's been back in my life. I'm damn proud of her for what she's accomplished, but I can't lie to Max and tell him it doesn't worry me she's a journalist. I witnessed her hesitation when we had dinner. She had to think about whether she was with me as a reporter or as a date.

There's a little whisper of doubt in the back of my mind that's urging me to slow down, but I can't.

It's that simple.

I want her.

I turn back to him. "I've thought about it. I'm going to talk with her when we're back and make sure we're on the same page about our professional lives not mixing with our personal ones."

"Do you think she'll be receptive to that? I mean, you'd be one hell of a story. Every sports journalist has been trying to get an interview with you for years. It'd be a hell of a step up for her career to be the reporter who lands you."

I glance away again, and this time I don't look back at him. I can't. He knows me too well and would be able to read the slight insecurity that's desperately trying to surface. It would absolutely make her career, but it would also be the end of us—permanently. When it comes to Paige, that's not the permanent I want. I'm just hoping she agrees.

TWENTY-FIVE

Paige

My knuckles rap against the sturdy wood door to Vince's office as I make my presence known. He's been in a million meetings this week, and every time I tried to meet with him, he seemed to disappear. As the days have dragged on, my patience has waned because I've been itching to talk to him about this Jack article.

I was naïve to think my feelings for Jack had been buried so deep that they wouldn't resurface as soon as we spent time together. Even when we've been apart, our conversations are richer than ever. I actually forgot what it felt like to laugh as hard as he's made me laugh the past couple of nights.

"Hey Vince, can I talk to you for a minute?"

He glances at me, his face lighting up. "Paige! Just the woman I wanted to see. How're things going with our favorite football player?"

"Um, good. Listen Vince, I really think it would be better if I focused my efforts on another article idea. I have several already started—"

He cuts me off. "Wait, are you still trying to get out of writing the Fuller piece? I thought we handled this weeks ago." He sits back in his chair, crossing his arms across his chest and looking at me like I just grew three heads and am speaking a language he doesn't understand.

"I told you I wasn't sure I was the right fit."

"Clearly you are, if Jack's response to you tells us anything. I've heard several people talking about it. There's a lot of buzz about you since that initial press conference. It's clear you two have chemistry. Just use that to your advantage."

He turns back to his computer like he's ready to dismiss me.

"I'm not sure I like what you're implying. I'm not the kind of reporter who gets...personal with her subjects." I'm not even going to bother telling him that Jack and I have been on a date and are talking regularly. The less fuel he has the better.

He scoffs. "I don't care what you do in your bedroom, Paige. I care about this story."

"I'm not doing it," I state.

He levels me with a hard glare, a similar look to the one he gave me last week when I was convinced he knew I was lying about Jack canceling our dinner plans. When he speaks, his tone is more menacing than I've ever heard from a boss before. "I will get this story, whether it's from you or from someone else."

His threat makes me pause. If someone else gets assigned to Jack, who knows what crap they could eventually dig up and throw out there. I mean, he hasn't shared anything that I think is particularly newsworthy—frankly, his life has been pretty consumed with football since college—but I've known of reporters in the past who twisted facts to fit their narrative. It's not a respected practice in the newspaper world, but it does happen. And it's not something I'm willing to let happen to Jack.

"Why do you want this story so badly? It doesn't even seem like something a paper as prestigious as the *Chronicle* would go after. It seems more like a TMZ story. You're not asking for a Barbara Walters interview; you're looking for an exposé. Why?"

"Don't be so naïve, Paige. Print media is dying. We're no longer competing with other newspapers or magazines; now we're competing with the average Joe who can break a story on social media and have it be trending within an hour.

"We need a major story, an exclusive, and nothing sells faster than something seedy. I don't care how I get it, but I will get a story on Jack Fuller. Our paper needs to be the one to finally get in front of everyone else instead of playing catch-up like we have been."

Vince's tenacity is infamous, but this is something else altogether. I can see in his eyes he's willing to do whatever it takes to get a Jack Fuller exclusive. My need to protect Jack from being taken advantage of becomes overwhelming. I know without a doubt that if I don't write this story, someone else will—someone with less than stellar intentions. At least if I write it, I can control the narrative. I can protect Jack from getting hurt like he did in college.

I nod at Vince. "Fine, I'll write it."

He sits back and examines me closely, and I fight against the urge to squirm.

He nods his head. "Glad to hear it."

With that, I get up and walk out of his office. I'll write an article, but it's not going to be a personal exposé on Jack. I'll find something that isn't well known but won't be completely tied to Jack. Something that'll appease Vince without jeopardizing my new and delicate relationship.

I'll figure this out. If I can't, then I'm not the reporter I thought I was.

Jack: Did you find your seat okay?
Me: Yes. ☺

Jack: Good. I'm glad you're here ☺

A giddy grin has been plastered on my face all day. The thought of finally getting to see him in person again makes my smile grow wider and shivers race down my arms. Talking to him every day has been absolute heaven. I guess I shouldn't really be that surprised. We were best friends for a decade before we ever started dating. That connection has always gone deep.

The only downside of talking every day is that the sexual tension is through the roof. My battery-operated boyfriend has been getting quite the workout this week. Just hearing Jack's voice sends tingles straight to my core and gets me so hot and bothered that I've stopped wearing underwear during our conversations because I just soak through them anyway.

I'm pulled from my sexual reverie when I notice the players rushing out onto the field, and the crowd goes wild with frantic cheering. I look to the field, searching for Jack. My gaze finds him almost instantly, and my body's reaction to him is immediate and more powerful than ever. He's so entirely male with his long, chiseled arms, broad chest, and lean frame. His dark brown hair accentuates his subtle tan, and I'm convinced he has to be the sexiest man I've ever laid eyes on.

A whisper echoes in the back of my mind that I shouldn't feel this strongly for him already after what we've been through, but I ignore it, choosing to listen to my heart instead of my head. The feelings he brings to life in me are ones I've been secretly longing for, and more than ever I don't want to tip this delicate balance that I've found myself in. But I also don't like keeping such a huge secret from him.

Please don't leave me when I tell you about the article.

My greatest fear is voiced as a quiet plea in my head. If I thought he broke me when he left me before, I know for a fact he'll thoroughly demolish my heart now.

I shove my fear aside, take a deep breath, and smile when I see him glance up at me. His face breaks into a dazzling grin that takes my breath away.

The game starts, and it quickly becomes clear who the winner will be. The Wolves get three touchdowns in the first quarter, leading their opponent 21-0. These are the worst games to watch—great for the fans who love a win, but so ridiculously boring. My favorite games are the nail-biters, the edge-of-your-seat ones where it comes down to the last minute.

By halftime, they're ahead 35-6. Jack seems relaxed as he jogs off the field next to one of his wide receivers—Edmonson, according to the jersey. The seats around me clear as people get up to go get food from concessions. I stay in my seat, engrossed in checking news updates on my phone.

The thought of my article still circles my head, and I open my notes app to think of possible alternatives that I could write about—things that no one else has mentioned but aren't a total invasion of his privacy. We've talked about so many different things during our late-night phone conversations, but most of it seems too personal to share with the world.

He's talked a few times about his work with a local high school football team, which I think has a lot of potential because I could also spotlight a low-income high school and garner some extra support for their football program. Nothing else that we've talked about has quite grasped my attention or stood out to me as a decent possibility.

I close out of the app and look around at the people left in the stands. It's fun to people watch when you're at a football game. There are vastly different personalities that congregate in the stands, and it can be highly entertaining to watch all the different antics of the various spectators.

I notice an elderly couple sitting a few rows up and to my right that are laughing and so clearly in love with each other.

The man leans in to whisper into his wife's ear, and at her nod, he quickly takes off his jacket and wraps it around her. A soft smile of contentment graces her face while he fusses over her and makes sure she's warm. My heart melts at the love that is so clear between them.

That could be Jack and me when we're old.

Ok, Paige, settle down. Getting a little ahead of yourself there. You guys haven't even talked about where this is heading yet.

A tap on my shoulder pulls me from my observation of the couple and my thoughts of the future. I turn to find Max, Jack's assistant, squatting near my seat.

"Hey, you busy?"

I quickly glance out at the empty field then turn back to him. "Nope. What's up?"

"Come with me. Someone is antsy to see you."

He rolls his eyes at his statement and then stands, looking down at me. My smile is wide as I hurriedly get up to follow him.

We pass several deserted hallways past the employee entrance, when suddenly a hand comes out of the nearest dark hallway and grasps mine. Before I can even voice my shock and fear, I'm pulled into the hall and chiseled arms wrap around my waist. I can make out Jack's smile in the dimness, and my racing heart begins to slow down.

"You almost gave me a heart attack," I scold him.

"I missed you. I thought we could make out in a deserted hallway like old times."

His whispered words transport me straight back to high school. Will he always make me feel like this? God, I hope so.

He brushes my hair away from my face. "Did you miss me?" There's the slightest hint of vulnerability in his gaze that keeps me from downplaying my feelings.

"You know I missed you," I whisper.

Our eyes lock, and I'm desperate to feel his lips on mine again. All those nights with

B.O.B. clearly did nothing because now that I can actually touch him, my body is vibrating with a yearning that is nearly consuming.

I reach up to wrap my hands behind his neck as he leans down and takes my mouth in a passionate kiss. The second our lips make contact, it's like fire explodes throughout my body. Our tongues explore each other's mouths while my hands grip his neck and his brush against my back, pulling me as close to him as he can with his pads in the way. His hands find their way to my ass, and he squeezes, letting out a groan that shoots another bolt of lust straight to my sex.

His mouth is hot against my neck, but I can hear his muttered words perfectly. "God, Paige. I want you so bad."

It's like a plea and a growl all at once. I'm pretty sure my heart has already soared out of my body from the desire lacing his words, and all I can do is mumble in agreement, my brain foggy with lust.

One of his hands slides up over my breast, and the moan that escapes my throat seems overly loud in this quiet hallway, but I can't find the will to care. I just want him to touch me everywhere.

"Jack," I plead, "I need you to touch me."

He lets out another tortured groan and then kisses me deeper, his mouth making love to mine while his hand slides down to the button of my jeans.

God, yes.

He quickly gets the button undone and the zipper down, and then plunges his hand down my panties, slipping a finger inside my wet heat.

"Fuck, you're soaked," he says with awe in his voice.

"Don't stop," I beg. I'm not even embarrassed about my behavior at this point—my need is fully in the driver's seat right now.

"Not a fucking chance," he growls.

He adds a second finger to the first, and that, combined with the friction of his palm against my clit has me soaring with the most spectacular orgasm I've had in a very long time.

My sensitive body trembles as I come down from my release, and he slides his hand back out. If this is what he can do to me with just his hand, I can't wait to see what he can do with the rest of his body.

His kiss turns soft and sweet. "Fuck, that was hot. I really need to get this thing under control," he insinuates with a glance down to his pants.

I laugh. "A little uncomfortable?" I ask, referring to the fact that he's wearing a cup which has very little give for his massive erection.

He huffs out a laugh. "Uh, yeah, just a bit." He rests his forehead on mine. "But it was worth it."

The sound of a throat being cleared, very loudly and obviously, interrupts us, and I try to quickly turn away so I can button my pants, but Jack angles himself so his body is blocking me from whoever's there.

I glance over to see one of the players—it looks like Edmonson. "Sorry to interrupt, but Coach is looking for you, Jack. He wants to talk to you about putting Briggs in for the third quarter since we're so far ahead."

Jack takes a deep, steadying breath. "Yeah, okay. Tell him I'll be there in a minute."

"Sure thing." Edmonson nods his head at me and then quickly walks away. As soon as he's out of sight, Jack turns back to me. Desire and longing still burn furiously in his eyes.

Wow, that's sexy.

It's a heady feeling to see how much he craves me. It's also incredibly arousing, despite the fact that I just had a glorious orgasm.

"I wish you didn't have to go," I whisper.

"Me too. Just so we're clear, we're going to finish this later."

I smile up at him. "Oh, I hope so."

His eyes light with mirth, although the need is still there too. Suddenly, his expression

becomes serious, and his voice is soft as he says, "I'm not letting you go this time."

He kisses me quickly and then walks backward toward the locker rooms. "I'll see you after the game."

He smirks at me, turns the corner, and disappears before I even get a chance to say something in response. I lean back against the wall, trying to brace myself after his promise. More than anything, I hope he's right. I desperately hope he won't let me go after I tell him about the article assignment.

TWENTY-SIX

Jack

I usually don't enjoy being benched but sitting on the sidelines gives me extra time to watch Paige while she watches the game. Coach Denton wanted to let our backup quarterback get some playing time in since we're so far ahead, and right now, I'm thankful for such a huge lead.

God, she's so fucking beautiful.

I could watch her all day and never tire of looking at her gorgeous and expressive face. I want so badly to tell her I still love her, maybe more now than before, but I don't want to freak her out. It's only been a couple of weeks since we got back together.

That's another thing we really need to talk about. We haven't discussed our relationship—whether or not we're officially a couple—but I think it's time. She needs to know she's the only woman I want. The team is going on the road again in a couple of days, and I don't want her thinking there will be other women on the side.

As far as I'm concerned, there will never be anyone else.

Movement on my right catches my attention, and I turn to see Will Edmonson sit down next to me. His expression is bleak, as usual. I don't think I've seen a smile on his face since before his fiancée, Candace, died in a drunk driving accident over a year ago. I spent weeks checking on him after it happened. He was in bad shape, and for a while, I was worried the darkness of his depression would consume him.

He and I bonded immediately when I first joined the Wolves. We've always been pretty good friends, but helping him get through the worst of his pain only strengthened that bond. He's one of the best guys I've ever met, and it kills me seeing him still struggle. I didn't truly understand, but now I look at him and all I can think about is what I would do if Paige died.

My stomach clenches painfully, and my chest feels tight at the thought. I look back up at the stands to assure myself that she's safe and push the horrible thought from my mind.

I have a new respect for what Will has gone through. I think Will Edmonson might just be the strongest person I know to go through all that and still get through every day.

He catches me looking at him. "Everything alright?" he asks.

"Yeah. Sorry. Zoned out for a minute."

"How're things going with your girl?"

I glance back at Paige. "Good. Really good. Great, actually." I can't help the grin that

spreads across my face and the warmth that floods my body simply thinking about Paige. Just seeing her sitting there, knowing she's here for me, still feels surreal sometimes.

"Do you love her?"

The question takes me by surprise. Will doesn't normally ask such personal questions—I suspect because he doesn't want anyone to turn the tables and ask him anything personal.

"Yeah, man, I do."

He nods once, then looks back out to the field. "Then don't let her go."

Looking back at the field, I reply, "I don't intend to."

I can see his smirk in my peripheral vision. Despite the shit that man has been through, he's happy for me. I glance behind me again to look at Paige one more time because I just can't help myself. She's staring at her phone, her brow furrowed in what's either frustration, concentration, or a combo of the two. Even from this distance, I can tell she's nibbling on the inside of her lip, which also tells me whatever she's thinking about is making her nervous. Cheering draws my attention back to the game, and I decide to ask her about it later. There's nothing I can do now anyway.

After the game, I emerge from the locker rooms, showered and clean, in a pair of jeans and my black fitted Henley with the sleeves pushed up. Paige sees me instantly, and desire pulses deep inside me when her gaze slides up and down my body, her eyes heating and her lips slightly parted.

I'm immediately taken back to the hallway during halftime. Fuck, she looked so damn sexy as she came on my fingers. My whole body is clamoring to be with her, to taste her on my tongue and feel her body as she convulses from her climax with me buried deep inside of her. She feels it too, if the heated look in her eyes is any indication.

The attraction has always been there, but it's different this time. Stronger. I've never felt this pull toward any woman other than Paige, but even back then, it wasn't quite like this. It's like it's matured and grown as we have.

I walk straight toward her, confidence in my steps and desire in my eyes. I need to feel her lips on mine. Right. Fucking. Now.

The moment I'm in front of her, I gently grab the back of her neck and draw her mouth to mine. Her body crushes against me, and she lets out the faintest moan in the back of her throat. I let out a low groan of my own as all the blood in my body rushes south.

Fuck, she tastes amazing. I can't get enough of this woman. I deepen the kiss, holding her close to me and loving the feel of her gripping my biceps like she's clinging to me for dear life.

A sound in the background brings me back to where we are, and I reluctantly tear my lips from hers. "We need to get out of here, or I'm going to end up taking you against this wall."

She lets out a breathless laugh. "I'd probably let you if you keep kissing me like that."

She looks up at me, and I'm left speechless. My God, she's so damn beautiful. Her cheeks are flushed, and her lips are red and swollen from my kisses.

"Okay, yeah, seriously, we need to get out of here. The last thing I need is for the media to snag a picture of us going at it against a wall," I say, grabbing her hand as we make our way toward the exit.

I'm glad I convinced her to take an Uber to the game because now I can keep touching her instead of being separated from her. I want as much time with her as I can get.

We make our way to my car, and I hold the passenger door open for her. She's quieter than normal, and I can't help but wonder if everything is okay. She seemed fine when she met me outside the locker room, but now it's like her mood has shifted.

I hop in the car and start driving toward my favorite pizza joint. I stumbled upon it when I first moved here and became friends with the owner, Antonio. He always makes sure I have my privacy from snoopy paparazzi, and he makes the best damn pizza in all of Los Angeles.

I glance toward Paige, who's staring out the passenger-side window looking lost in her own thoughts. I can just barely catch her reflection in the glass as we drive past streetlights, and the worried expression on her face immediately puts me on guard.

"You okay?"

She turns to me and smiles, although it doesn't reach her eyes. "Yeah, I'm fine. I'm just kind of tired, and I think I might be coming down with something. Can we take a raincheck on dinner?"

I'm a little surprised by her request. "Uh, sure. Do you want to maybe come back to my place? We can just hang out together. I'd really like to spend some time with you before I head out of town again."

She almost looks guilty when she replies, "I really think I should just go home. If I am coming down with something, I don't want you to get it before you go on the road."

Disappointment seeps through me, but I cover it quickly with a nod of my head. "Yeah, okay. I'll take you home."

"Thanks," she mumbles, turning her head to look back out her window.

I navigate through downtown toward her apartment, worry gnawing at my gut. Paige is lying. She was never very good at it, and knowing her as well as I always have, I can see all the signs. The way she won't make eye contact and nibbles on her lip while she restlessly messes with her hands. I can't help but wonder if this has something to do with her job. My mind shifts back to our last dinner date when she hesitated. Is she still questioning where her loyalties lie?

"Can I ask you something?"

She turns toward me. "Sure."

I hesitate, thinking about how I want to phrase this. "I know your job is really important to you."

"It is," she confirms.

"And you know that my privacy is really important to me." I briefly glance over at her, but it's long enough to see guilt shadow her face. My stomach clenches.

She finally responds, "I do."

I decide just to spit it out. "My question is this—are we in agreement that we'll keep our professional lives separate from our personal lives?"

I can feel her eyes on me, but it doesn't soothe the fear that's stirring in my belly at her lack of response.

"Can I ask a question of my own?"

"You still haven't answered mine," I point out.

"I will, I promise, but I would really like the answer to mine before I answer yours."

"Okay, shoot."

"Where do you see this going with us?"

Without hesitation, I respond, "I want us to be exclusive. I have no intention of dating anyone else, and I'd like the same assurances from you."

"Okay. I can do that. Anything else?"

"I just want to be with you, Paige. Any way you'll have me." That's a lie. I want to marry this woman, without a doubt in my mind. She's it for me.

I glance at her in time to see her smile at my response. "I can think of lots of ways that I'd like to have you."

Her smile turns saucy, and while I'd love nothing more than to play along, I need an answer.

"So, are you going to answer my question now?"

Her tone turns serious. "Jack, I will always look out for you. I agree that we should keep our work separate from our relationship." She hesitated only a moment before she answered, but it was long enough that I don't feel entirely comforted by her response.

Before I can push deeper into the conversation, I pull up at her apartment. I park the car, walk her to her door, and give her a brief kiss before heading back out into the warm LA night. It's almost ten p.m., but it's still pretty warm for October.

I look up toward the window of her apartment and see her lights on, but she's not standing by the window like I wish she was. I also wish I knew what she was thinking and why she lied to me about not wanting to go out tonight. This is an aspect of our relationship that's new to me, and I hate it. We never kept secrets before. Paige always confided in me about everything.

I get back in my car, processing the conversation we just had. I want to trust what she said, but there was something in her tone and expression that has my defenses rising. And I can't help wondering—can I trust Paige?

TWENTY-SEVEN

Paige

My back lands heavily on my bed, disturbing the clothes I flung haphazardly on the unmade sheets when I tried to find the perfect outfit for tonight. Hot tears of frustration slide down my cheeks because I have no idea how to navigate my way through this situation. His comment about not wanting the media to snap a picture of us when we were in the hall was like being doused with ice water. If only he knew the truth and that the journalist he should maybe be most concerned about is the one he was kissing.

Even though I'd love nothing more than to spend time with him tonight, my guilt is overwhelming me, and I'm worried that if I tell him about my assignment, he'll back off. My poor heart can't handle his rejection a second time. Hell, I wasn't even sure it would survive the first time. I became a more reserved, distant version of the girl I was after Jack broke up with me all those years ago. But the past few weeks with him, I've felt lighter, carefree, like I was shedding the skin I'd been wearing for so long and embracing the woman I was always supposed to be. I'm not ready to lose that.

How the hell did I get myself into this impossible situation?

Actually, the better question is how can I get out of it without losing the job I've worked so hard for, or the man who's always had my heart?

Groaning, I roll over and grab my phone from my purse on the floor. I speed-dial the one person who will hopefully be able to offer me some clarity in this clusterfuck that I'm living.

Gina answers after the first ring. "Hey, what's up?"

"I need your advice. I'm starting to go a little crazy here."

"Advice about what?"

"Jack. And my boss. And how the hell I'm supposed to write this article while I'm falling in love with the subject. I'm terrified he'll break things off as soon as he finds out, especially after the conversation we just had—"

"Girl, you need to slow way the hell down," she cuts me off. First of all, let me correct you on one point. You are not falling in love with that man. You've been in love with him since you were sixteen, probably longer than that. Yes, he broke your heart, but you still loved him. That's why no other guy has ever stuck for you."

She can't see me nod my head, but she's right. "Okay, I'll give you that. Go on."

"Okay, now to the article thing. I think you should just tell him. Explain the situation to him. I'm sure he'll understand the position you're in. Who knows, maybe he'd even be down to do an interview with you."

I roll my eyes and sigh heavily. "I think you're wrong. You didn't hear his voice tonight."

"What are you talking about?"

"He asked me straight up if we were on the same page about keeping our personal lives and professional lives separate. That doesn't sound like someone who would be willing to give me an exclusive."

"Hmm." She pauses before finally saying, "maybe he would if you told him about Vince."

I roll my face into my pillow, letting out another groan. "Ugh, this situation feels impossible. If I don't write the article, then Vince will make my life at the paper hell and probably get a story on Jack anyway. But if I tell Jack about the article, I feel like he's going to completely shut down and pull away. You didn't see his face, Gina. It's clear he doesn't want me to write about him, or us, not that I'd write about us anyway. I never put myself in my pieces; you know that."

She hums an affirmative.

Thinking about his face during our conversation forces a horrible thought into my head. "What if I bring it up, and he thinks I only got back together with him for this stupid article? It might make him question my intentions, and the last thing I want is for him to doubt how sincere my feelings are for him."

"You're going to give yourself an ulcer stressing about it. Despite your fears, I still think your best bet is to talk to Jack and just get everything out there. If he thinks you got back together simply for that article, then he doesn't know you at all. And if he lets you go over that, then he certainly doesn't deserve you. Tell him you're in love with him and want to have all his babies. That should thoroughly distract him from the whole article debacle."

"Gina! If I actually said that to him, I'd probably see a Jack-shaped hole in my wall. It's way too soon to even go there. We only just established that we are, in fact, a couple again."

I can't jeopardize my relationship with Jack. Yet, the only reason I even accepted this assignment was to protect him since Vince is dead set on getting an exposé on him. I chew my bottom lip, trying to solve this problem in my head.

"I can literally hear your brain overthinking and overana-lyzing through the phone. Stop it right now."

Gina knows me too well. It's inconvenient at times like this, when I'm prepared to wallow in my misery.

"Listen, Gina, I gotta go. I need to think some things through."

"Go soak in a bubble bath, think about that hot hunk of man you're seeing, and call me tomorrow. Love you, girl! Everything will work out in the end. Keep your chin up."

I hang up the phone, roll out of my bed, and walk to my window. I stare at the lights of downtown and the chaos on the roads that seems to mirror the chaos in my head. Turning on my heel, I quickly decide to take Gina's advice and soak in a lavender bath until I settle down a little.

After a restless night's sleep, I walk into work, coffee in hand, sunglasses still on, and my purse slung over my shoulder. I'm just about to reach my desk when my boss calls my name. I turn to Vince and see him motion for me to come into his office. He turns away before I can ask him to give me a second to put my stuff down.

Cocky, arrogant bastard.

I try to rein in my irritation. I do not function well on little sleep.

Alicia walks by my desk and offers a small sympathetic smile. "Looks like Vince is on a tear this morning. He's already laid into three people, and the day has barely started."

"Fantastic," I mutter as I hastily set my stuff down on my desk before rushing into his office. "You wanted to see me?"

Without looking up from the papers scattered on his desk, he responds, "Yeah, how's the story on Jack Fuller coming along?"

"It's a work in progress."

He glances up and eyes me carefully. "Do I need to reiterate how important this piece will be to the success of our paper?"

I look him boldly in the eye, determined not to show how weak I'm feeling when it comes to this story. "No, you do not."

"I'd really hate to have to pass this off to someone else." His words have the slightest hint of irritation.

I force down my own annoyance. "I already told you I'd write the article. There's no need to put anyone else on it."

He nods slowly, but his words are anything but reassuring. "Alright then. You keep working on that. I want to see some decent notes by the end of the week."

I nod sharply, holding my tongue for fear that I'll say something snarky.

"You can go now." He looks back down at his papers, clearly dismissing me like the condescending ass that he is.

Frustrated, I retreat to my desk, hoping I can find some way to maneuver through this minefield I am currently standing in. If I give my boss exactly what he wants, I'm betraying Jack's trust in me. But if I don't give him anything, then I could possibly lose the career that I've worked my ass off for. I need to find a middle ground—fast—and solidify the focus of my article.

I decide to focus on the local high school football program that Jack helps out with. After several hours of writing down everything I can remember from my conversations with Jack and researching the school's history and their program, I decide I deserve a break.

I grab my purse and walk out of the building, deeply inhaling the warm fresh air and feeling the heat of the sun on my skin. Only twenty seconds outside and I already feel better. My head is clearer, and the weight of this article no longer seems like such a burden. I make my way slowly down the street toward the Starbucks on Maple. While I wait for my drink to be made, I hear my cell phone buzzing in my purse. I quickly answer the call as soon as I see my mom's name on the caller ID.

"Hey, Mom."

"Hi, sweetie. I was just calling to see how you're doing. We haven't had a chance to talk since you got all settled in your new apartment. How are you liking LA?"

My mom and I are close and normally talk a lot more frequently, but with everything that has happened at work and then with Jack, I haven't quite caught her up on the happenings of my life.

"LA is good. Crowded and busy, but good." I grab my drink that is now ready and head outside to sit. "Work has been stressful."

I don't know why I'm hesitating to tell my mom all that's going on. She'd been supportive of Jack and me when we were teens and first started dating. Maybe I'm hesitant because she saw the aftermath of that love. She watched her only daughter emotionally fall apart, before I eventually toughened up and shut many of those emotions off altogether. She saw the way losing Jack changed me. I'm afraid she won't be as supportive this time around.

"I, uh, saw Jack." I wait with bated breath for a reaction, a noise, anything. Silence fills the line. "Mom, are you there?"

Calmly, and with what sounds oddly like mild amusement, she remarks, "Jack Fuller?"

"Yeah."

"And how did that go? How's he doing?"

"He's great. He's the quarterback for the Wolves now."

"Oh, I know all that, honey. Your father filled me in on that when he first got drafted."

Shocked, I reply, "Dad? He's been following Jack's career?" I always thought I was the only one in my family that still followed what Jack was doing.

"You know how your father loves football. So…" She hesitates, and my stomach clenches, waiting for her next question. "How was it seeing Jack again?"

I remember the way our eyes locked on each other when he was lying on the field and then that kiss in the hallway that turned positively indecent, and all the wonderful moments in between.

On a breath, I whisper, "It's been…incredible."

I take another deep breath and let it all out. I tell her all about the press conference, the hike, our date, and how we've talked every day since.

"I knew you two would find a way back to each other."

"What?" I'm shocked. I thought she would question my judgment, but all I hear in her tone is the amusement I thought I heard earlier.

"You two always belonged together. It was hard when we moved, watching you two struggle, and then when you broke up, my heart hurt so much for you, Paige. But I always thought, if you two just got in the same room again, you would get back together. You were too young to make it work back then, but you're both older and more mature now. And you're back in the same city. It's like it was meant to be."

"I never pegged you as a hopeless romantic, Mom. I'm kind of surprised."

"Well, I'm not usually, but in this case, it's not hopeless romance, it's hopeful. I always had hope that you two would find a way back to each other. People don't take young love very seriously, but what you and Jack had wasn't simply young love. It was real, and it was stronger than what most people find as adults.

"I'm glad you two are working through things. Jack was a good boy, and from what I've seen in the media, or maybe what I haven't seen, if you know what I mean, he's turned into a good man."

"He is a good man, Mom."

"I thought so. You sound happy, Paige."

I smile, thinking of Jack's arms wrapped around me. "I am happy, for the most part."

"For the most part? Are there other things going on?" The motherly concern is evident in

her voice.

Despite my initial intention of leaving all the drama out of this conversation, I decide to spill the whole mess with my boss to my mom. Her advice is the same as Gina's. She urges me to talk to Jack, the sooner, the better.

"Well, I need to get going. I have to run some errands before making dinner. Call us a little more frequently if you can. You know we worry about you."

"I will, Mom. Love you."

"Love you too." With that, she hangs up.

I continue to sit on the cement bench under the tree right outside Starbucks. As I soak up

the fading sun, I realize that all my tension faded away as soon as I started talking about Jack. He's what's important, and I need to protect him in any way I can. I'll make the philanthropy angle work and let Jack read it before it goes to print. That way he'll know my intentions were good from the start, and I'll save my job—hopefully.

With strengthened determination, I head back to the office.

TWENTY-EIGHT

Jack

Three days shouldn't feel like three months, but it sure as fuck does when it's three days away from Paige. After our failed pizza date, I decided to give her a day before texting her to check in. Frankly, I needed the time to ease my growing concern about where her loyalties lie— with me or the paper. But then I got busy with football obligations, and my only form of communication was a text here and there.

Tonight's the first night I've finally had a chance to call her, and I'm dying to talk to her. As soon as she answers the phone, her sweet voice soothes the insecurity that was stirring in my gut only a few days ago.

"Hey," she answers softly, her voice calming me in a way I didn't even know I needed.

"Hey, how are you?"

"Good." She exhales heavily. "I'm sorry about the other night, Jack."

I pause before responding hesitantly, "Sorry for what exactly?"

"Well, a couple of things, really, but mainly the awkwardness that was there when you dropped me off."

"Paige, I want to be with you. There's no doubt in my mind. Do you want to be with me?" Because at the end of the day, that's all that matters.

"Yes," she responds instantly.

There's still one thing holding me back from feeling completely relaxed with her again. "I know your career is important to you, and I can admire that, but I need to know you'll be able to keep your career separate from us. Can you do that?"

"You're right, my career is important to me. Honestly, it used to be the most important thing to me."

"Used to be?"

"It's not anymore," she whispers. "Jack, please don't doubt that I will always do whatever I can to protect you and put you first. I'm in this. I want to be with you."

I close my eyes, allowing her words to wash over me and bring me the relief I've been searching for.

Coming back to our conversation, I say, "You mentioned there was more than one thing you were sorry for. What else is there?"

She giggles, and fuck me, that sound is so sexy coming from her.

"We didn't get to finish what we started during halftime," she states seductively.

And just like that, I'm hard.

My voice is hoarse when I speak, "You're right, we didn't. What are you wearing right now?"

She laughs. "You want to do this now?"

"Hey, you're the one who started it," I tease.

It's a weird sensation to be hard as stone and laughing with her. It's never been like this with anyone else. It feels good.

Her laugh quiets on the other end of the line. "Do you want the truth? Or something sexy?"

I smirk at her adorableness. "I always want the truth."

"I'm wearing a tank top and yoga pants."

I groan, picturing her in my head. "God, I bet you still look sexy as hell." I think about how her ass felt in my hands the other night, and my hand slides into my boxer briefs, gripping my now rigid length.

"What are you wearing?" Her voice is soft but not tentative. She's feeling this too.

"Just my boxer briefs."

"Take them off," she demands.

Fuck, that's hot. I love this side of Paige. I remove my hand from my cock and slide my boxer briefs down my legs. "I think it's only fair if I'm naked that you should be, too."

I swear I can hear her smile through the phone. "I already am."

I can't stop the groan that releases from my mouth. "Touch yourself," I beg inelegantly.

Honestly, I don't even care where she touches herself because I can already imagine how sexy she looks, stroking her hands over her breasts and then down to caress her slick heat. When she lets out a breathy moan, I think I might lose my fucking mind with how badly I want this woman.

"Fuck, babe, tell me what you're doing that just had you making that sexy-ass sound."

Her breathing is erratic and her voice husky when she responds, "I'm touching my breast with one hand and the other is rubbing my clit. I want you to touch yourself."

"I already am," I state, using her line from earlier. This woman has me strung so damn tight, but this already feels better than all the times I've jacked off since we got back together.

My balls tighten, release imminent. "Fuck, Paige, I'm gonna come. I need you to come with me."

"Yes," she breathes out and releases another loud moan.

We pant into the phone together as we find our release. When both our breathing has finally evened out, she huffs out a laugh. "Well, can't say I've ever done that before."

I laugh with her as I look down at the mess covering my stomach and pecs. "Uh, yeah, that was a first for me too."

"Really?" She seems surprised.

"Yeah, really. I was never really a playboy like everyone wants to think. That carried too much risk of unwanted exposure."

She's quiet for a minute before finally responding, determination clear in her voice, "I know your privacy is important to you, Jack. I won't betray your trust."

And just like that, my insecurities about her loyalties get tucked away. "I trust you, Paige."

Ever since that night of phone sex, I've been dying to get her in my bed. Knowing I can't wait any longer to have her, I decided to do something extra special for our date today. Paige has made it clear that she's ready to take that next step, but I still want it to be special. I want it to mean something.

I pick her up and drive us out to San Pedro. It's a beautiful Southern California day with clear skies and the perfect temperature.

"So, are you going to tell me where we're going?" Paige asks. Her head is leaning back on the headrest but turned toward me with the most gorgeous smile on her face.

I glance at her quickly with a mischievous smile. "I told you, it's a surprise."

"So, not even a hint?"

"Nope."

She leans over and whispers, "What if I do this?"

I feel her teeth graze my ear and I can't hold back my moan. "Paige," I warn.

I look over at her and see her eyes dancing with mirth. I love this playful side of her, but damn, it's distracting and making me hornier than ever. She places her hand right above my knee, and I'm forced to take a deep breath as I try to control my impulse to pull the car over and ravage her right now. I start counting the ABCs backward to tame the growing issue in my pants and cool down my lust. When her hand starts sliding up my thigh, I quickly stop her with my own.

"Paige, please. I'm trying to be a gentleman here, but you're making it really hard."

She giggles. "Oh, I can tell."

I throw my head back and let out another groan. Immediately, I lose the heat of her palm on my thigh as she moves her hand back to her own lap, laughing softly. But just as I start to relax and calm my breathing, she leans over and whispers, "Maybe I don't want you to be a gentleman."

The heat in her eyes is almost my undoing. How the fuck did I ever let her go for so long?

I'm saved from my thoughts and from having to respond to Paige's comment because we pull up to our destination, Point Fermin Park. I park along the street, the main attraction still hidden behind the trees filling the park. I can see a hint of white, but that's about it. Nerves start to fill my gut. I hope she likes this. I haven't exactly been the most romantic guy since we split years ago. She was the only woman I ever really wanted to be romantic with, so I'm massively out of practice.

"Wait here."

I jump out of the car and hustle over to her side. I see her eyes light up and her lips quirk up at the corners in a smile as I open her door. She takes the hand I offer her and slides out of the car. Once she's out, I go around back and grab a blanket and picnic basket from the trunk.

"Wow, you really went all out, didn't you?" There's a musicality to her voice that tells me she's pleased by this simple gesture.

"I told you I wanted our date to be special," I tell her as I walk back to her.

She cups my cheek. "You don't need to go to any trouble to make it special, Jack. Just being with you is enough."

She goes up on her toes and kisses me sweetly, her lips the gentlest caress against mine.

I forgot about this feeling. This euphoria that spreads through my whole body and leaves me tingling and wanting more. She's the only woman who's ever elicited this reaction from me, who's ever made me feel this way.

I rest my forehead on hers. "Come on. The picnic basket isn't the surprise."

I lead her down the sidewalk, along the pathway that leads to the main reason I chose this location. As we walk hand in hand, the white base of the building comes into view. I glance at Paige to watch her reaction. She's looking around the park, taking everything in, and then catches me looking at her. She smiles at me before her gaze catches the building in front of us as we finally clear the trees, and she realizes what she's seeing.

She slows, and a heavy breath leaves her lungs. "Jack...I had no idea this was here."

The Point Fermin Lighthouse stands tall before us, glowing white from the bright sunshine. She continues to look in awe at the building as we walk toward the entrance. I'm captivated as I watch her face light up. She looks radiant.

We take a private tour of the building, looking out at the beautiful views of the Pacific Ocean. Afterward, I set up our picnic on the grass nearby.

She shakes her head. "I can't believe you brought me to a lighthouse for our date."

"Lighthouses were always our thing. At least the one back home. We had a lot of firsts there."

I smile at the blush that spreads across her cheeks, evidence that she clearly remembers when we had our first kiss, as well as losing our virginity together, at the lighthouse at Chinook Point.

"I remember," she replies softly.

She gently places her palm on my cheek and guides my face to hers. Her kiss is soft and slow but filled with so much emotion, it nearly makes my heart stop. I wish I could press pause and live in this moment forever.

We spend a couple of hours sitting and talking while admiring the gorgeous views. Miracle of miracles, I only get a couple of requests for autographs, which fortunately doesn't kill the mood. When I offer up the idea of going back to my place, Paige doesn't hesitate.

"I'd love to."

My nerves don't kick in until we get through the entrance of my gated community and pull up to my house. It's not as large as some of the guys' houses on my team, but it sure as hell isn't small either. I'm nervous to see her reaction to the one place that has become my sanctuary.

I pull the car into the garage and we make our way through my mudroom into the connecting kitchen.

"Want a tour?"

She nods her head, her eyes soaking up every detail of my house. The main floor is open-concept, so she can see the dining room and living room from our spot in the kitchen. I steer her down a hallway that leads us to the front door and a large staircase. The staircase leads to the upstairs where most of the bedrooms are, including mine, but I'm not ready to have her so close to my room.

Well, scratch that, I'm more than ready. But I don't intend to jump on her the second I get her in my house. And by looking at her, it doesn't seem like she's ready for that.

Actually, it looks like she's massively uncomfortable. Anyone else might think she was just looking around, but I know her. I can see the tension in her shoulders and around her eyes and mouth. She's uncomfortable.

Shit.

My heart drops to my stomach. I want her to be happy here, so I need to fix this pronto. I quickly finish up the tour, breezing past the game room, personal gym, and infinity pool that takes up half of my sprawling back patio. I lead her back to the kitchen and offer her a drink, while I quickly place a delivery order for dinner through an app on my phone.

She nods but still doesn't say anything. Silence descends heavily on us, feeling like a weighted blanket but without the comfort. I hand her a glass of red wine while I sip on my two fingers of whiskey.

She walks toward the wall of windows that overlooks the pool outside and the view of LA. Finally breaking the silence, she turns with a coy smile that doesn't quite reach her eyes.

"This is an incredible view. I bet this pool is one hell of a chick magnet."

I shrug. "I wouldn't know. I've never brought a woman here." We don't break eye contact as she turns her body toward me.

"What?" It's a whisper from her lips as if she can't believe the truth.

I slowly make my way toward her, placing my drink on the counter as I move from the kitchen.

"I've never brought another woman here before. This place is my sanctuary away from all the bullshit. I haven't had a serious relationship since college, definitely not the whole time

I've been in the NFL. There are too many jersey chasers. And as you know, I like my privacy. I bought this house after my first season. The only people who've been here are my parents, Max, and a few of the guys from the team."

I pause to assess if she's ready to hear what I'm about to say.

With my voice strong and sure, I state, "I only bring people that really matter here. You're the only woman who's ever mattered."

She takes an audible breath, sets her wine glass on the table next to the couch, and walks over to me. As soon as she's within arm's reach, I slide my fingers through her hair and grasp the back of her neck, drawing her lips to mine.

The second we connect, it's like electricity hums through my veins. Her fingers curl around my neck, gripping my hair. When she tugs on the short hairs there, I can't contain the groan that spills from my throat. That sound is like a starting gun going off, and our kiss turns ravenous, like we can't get enough of each other.

"God, I want to taste every inch of you," I breathe out, my voice husky with desire.

I find that tender spot on her neck that always gets her worked up, and the moan that releases from her mouth is complete seduction. It's audio porn, making me harder than granite at the idea that she's mine and mine alone. No one else gets to have her this way or make her crazy out of her mind with desire the way I do.

I break our kiss, grab her hand, and walk her to my room upstairs. I don't want our first time together in almost a decade to be on my couch.

The moment we pass the threshold of my room, I spin her around and press her against the wall. My lips capture hers in a deep, possessive kiss.

Her moan damn near unmans me.

Her fingers slip under my shirt and claw against my lower back.

"I wanted this to be slow and sweet, but I don't think I can wait," I whisper.

"Fuck slow. I want you so badly."

She kisses me deeply, her fingers moving up my body to grip my hair again. I'm overwhelmed by my need for her. I pull my lips from hers just long enough to rip off her shirt and mine before we're connected again.

Our mouths move together in a dance of passion and need. I move my hand around her back to release the clasp of her bra, while her hands move toward the button on my pants. Through gasping breaths, demanding kisses, and short bursts of laughter, we struggle to get out of the remainder of our clothes. But the second I see her standing in front of me fully naked, all the laughter stops.

She's the most breathtaking woman I've ever seen.

I slide my hand around the back of her neck, through her hair, and bring her mouth to mine, devouring her with everything I have. I'm desperate for her to feel all the emotions rolling through my body in this moment. I lift her up into my arms, her legs wrapping around my hips, and walk toward my bed without disconnecting our lips.

Once I lay her back on my bed, I move my lips back to that sensitive spot on her neck, and I watch in delight as goosebumps appear on her skin and she moans softly in my ear. I slide my lips down, determined to kiss every inch of her gorgeous body.

She's fuller than she was when we were teens, but in the most seductive way possible. Her body is the body of a woman, not a girl, and I'm so fucking turned on, I don't know if I'll last long once I slide into her warm, wet pussy.

I slide my tongue across her nipple and watch her as she arches her back up into me, a quiet gasp falling from her lips. I suck it into my mouth, hard, just to hear her gasp louder. Then I slide my mouth over to the other side and give her other nipple the same treatment.

Her body writhing underneath mine is not helping me any, and I'm dangerously close to coming already just from the feel of her skin against mine. I pull back and rest my forehead on her stomach, taking deep breaths while trying to control my raging hard-on.

Fuck, I don't think I've been this hard in my entire life. I feel like this is becoming a pattern with Paige.

Her fingers slide into my hair again, and I lift my head to look into her gorgeous brown eyes.

"Jack, I need you. I need you inside me right now."

"I need to grab a condom."

"Do you?" she asks quietly.

"Do I?" I repeat, not quite believing what she's suggesting, but hoping it's what I think it is. I've never gone without a condom before, but Paige is definitely the woman I'd make an exception for.

"I'm on the pill and clean. I was checked at my last annual appointment and haven't been with anyone since."

"I'm clean. I haven't been with anyone in almost a year and was clean when I had my physical three months ago."

"Good. Because I really want to feel you bare inside me."

Her words are my undoing. I move to kiss her and slide inside her just as our lips touch. We both moan loudly at the exquisite feeling of being coupled together.

There is nothing in the world like being inside Paige, but to feel her with no barrier between us is beyond anything I've ever experienced.

I move inside her, trying to hold myself back because I'm seriously in danger of coming like a virginal teen boy getting his dick wet for the first time.

"Paige," I groan. "Fuck, you feel so goddamn good."

"Jack," she moans breathlessly, "I'm so close already."

I move my hand down between us to rub her clit while I continue to thrust inside her. Her

back arches, and she screams my name as her orgasm hits her. Her wet heat squeezing me as she comes is my complete undoing, and I come hard, her insides milking me through my own climax.

Completely spent, I adjust our bodies so we're side by side, facing each other, yet still touching almost entirely while we take deep breaths and recover from the best sex I've ever had.

TWENTY-NINE

Paige

My chest heaves as I lie there, still breathless from the most incredible orgasm I've ever had. I look into Jack's face and see an expression of complete contentment that must mirror my own.

"Wow."

Jack huffs out a laugh. "You can say that again." His eyes soften as he slides the hair off my forehead and tucks it behind my ear. "Watching you come is still the hottest thing I've ever seen."

My heart stutters as I remember those words whispered after we had sex for the first time as teens. I cup his face and kiss him softly, all the pain and hurt of our past seemingly being healed with this one kiss.

I love you.

The words shout in my head, but I can't say them yet. An alert goes off on Jack's phone and he reaches over.

"That's the security gate. Looks like our food is here. I'll be right back." He kisses me quickly and jumps out of bed, grabs a pair of sweats from his dresser, and then leaves the room. I sit up, wanting to put some clothes on while we eat, and decide to rummage through his closet to borrow one of his shirts.

He has a massive walk-in closet that seems way more organized than I remember him being. Just when I'm about to turn toward the drawers and look for a T-shirt, I notice a familiar-looking sleeve. The leather is still butter soft and I remember all the times I walked down the hallway holding Jack's hand while he wore this jacket.

I pull it from the hanger and slide my arms through it. The bottom edge of the jacket falls almost indecently high on my thighs. It just barely conceals my most intimate part, but the rest of the jacket is insanely big on me.

I hear Jack come back into the room talking about how he brought me my abandoned wine from earlier and some water to go with our Chinese food. I come out of the closet just as he turns around, and I watch his jaw drop as he scans me from head to toe. I'm standing before him wearing his high school letterman jacket, and only his jacket. My cheeks heat as I watch his pants begin to tent.

He clears his throat. "Fuck. You are every wet dream I ever had come to life."

His voice is gravelly with desire, and his look of shock has quickly been replaced with a ravenous one. He walks slowly toward me, his hand sliding over his mouth and jaw before he slides it through his hair. His eyes roam across my body from my head to my toes and back again.

"Do you know how many times I imagined this exact picture in my head? I always wondered what you would look like wearing just this jacket." He strokes his finger down the inside of the lapel and grazes the edge of my breast. "You look better than anything I ever fantasized."

His lips graze mine in a soft kiss that quickly consumes us both. He breaks away, breathing heavily. "Come on. Let's go eat before I ravage you again."

He smirks at me and grabs my hand, walking us to the bed

where he's laid down a towel and placed our Chinese food containers. We eat and talk, sharing more memories from our childhood and teenage years.

When the food is gone, we cuddle and continue talking, sharing our dreams and desires. I wish I could capture this moment and hold it close to my heart forever.

This night is more perfect than any dream.

Our soft touches become more sensual until Jack is kissing every inch of slowly exposed skin. He takes his time removing his letterman jacket from my body and then drives me insane as his tongue makes its way slowly to my clit, while two fingers slide into my already wet core. He uses his other hand to hold down my hips as he takes me over the peak with his fingers and tongue.

My God, the things that man can do with his mouth should be illegal.

He slides back up my body after my tremors have finally ceased and kisses me fiercely. The taste of myself in his kiss is a heady and erotic mix, and it isn't long before I flip him over and take my time devouring his body.

He grips my hair when I take him in my mouth, not to push me farther down, but just to touch me. He doesn't take over, but instead just holds on as I take him toward the peak.

He grabs me under my arms and pulls me up his body before rolling us over in the blink of an eye. He slides into me before I even have a chance to ask why he stopped me, and we both moan at the bliss of being connected again.

Jack takes me slowly this time, and I revel in our connection as he makes love to me with everything he has. Our eyes never break their hold on each other, even when we both crash over the peak of our climaxes. It's the most powerful sexual experience I've ever had, and I know without a doubt that after tonight we'll never be the same.

THIRTY

Jack

I had a girlfriend once who made me watch *500 Days of Summer* with her. As I walk into practice, I can't help but feel like Joseph Gordon-Levitt in the scene right after he and Zooey Deschanel have sex for the first time. I'm all smiles and on cloud nine as I walk into the locker room to get changed.

Practice is long and grueling, but I'm still feeling really good when we finish. I'm pounding a Gatorade when I see Max walking over.

"Hey man, how's it going? Any updates I need to know about?" I ask him.

"Nah, not really. There were a few more reporters I had to keep out. Another female reporter hoping she could catch your eye and snag a story." He looks out at the other players still working out on the field. "You know, I didn't really make the connection until just recently, but Paige was one of those female reporters I turned away awhile back. It was before that game where you saw her in the stands."

My gut clenches, and I turn to look at my friend closely. "You're telling me you think Paige was at the stadium trying to get a story on me?"

"Yeah, I'm sure it was her, man. I have no reason to lie to you. Trust me, I didn't want to say anything. For what it's worth, I think what you two have is the real deal, but I also wouldn't be doing my job or being a good friend if I didn't tell you."

I look at my friend, whom I trust with my life, and I can't help the little nugget of doubt about Paige that stirs back up and settles deep in my belly. I start replaying all our interactions and conversations since we first saw each other over a month ago. If she was writing a story, she'd have plenty of personal details. I haven't held anything back from her—not since our first date—despite that voice in the back of my head that wonders if I can really trust her or not.

Belatedly, I realize Max has been talking to me. "What did you say?"

He looks at me for a moment before repeating himself. "I said, I've never gotten the vibe that she was digging around for information on you. Every time I've seen you two interact, it seems genuine. She's never asked me any personal questions about you. Hell, she's never really asked me ANY questions about you. If she's writing a story, I would think she'd dig around. That's what the other reporters have tried to do. I don't really think you have anything to worry about, but I'll keep an ear out regardless."

I think about what he's just said and then my brain goes back to last night. None of that felt fake. Every incredible moment of last night was real. I'd bet my career on it. Like Max, I've never felt like Paige was digging. If anything, the more I think about it, the more I realize that Paige usually hates talking about work.

But what if she doesn't want to talk about it because I'm her story? That nugget of doubt in my stomach gets a little bigger.

"Let me know if you hear anything. I expect the paparazzi will pick up the news that we're dating sooner or later, but anything else about us, or about me, specifically from the *Chronicle*, I want to know about."

"How ironic is it that the NFL's most private player would fall for a journalist? Do you think she'd really write a story about you?"

I hesitate before speaking. "I wish I could say I was sure that she wouldn't, but the truth is I don't know."

The guilt that comes with that comment takes me by surprise. I shouldn't be doubting Paige. She's never given me a reason to doubt her loyalty.

"You know what? No, I don't think she'd write a story about me. She's never been like that, and in the month we've been together, she's been open and honest about her life. She told me she was going to keep our personal lives separate from our work lives, and I trust her."

He nods his head, like this is the reaction he expected. "I'll support you no matter what."

"Thanks, man. I'm gonna head to the locker room to shower and change." I pat him on the back and head to the showers.

As the water pours over my body, I realize that despite what I told Max, doubt has made itself comfortable in my gut, and now I can't shake the feeling that maybe Paige is hiding something from me.

THIRTY-ONE

Paige

Work drags on at a snail's pace as I sit at my desk working on my article. There's been very little press about the philanthropic aspect of Jack's life. Everyone else has been focused on his romantic ties or if there were more scandalous aspects of his personal life.

I've not found any articles discussing how he supports a local high school football team in South Central LA. He even shared with me how he goes there at least once a month to work out with the boys and typically once a week during their season.

My plan is to focus on the school and the football program, maybe even do some player profiles, and share it with Jack when it's ready so I can get his approval before I submit it to Vince. I don't want it to be solely about him, but I think it'll be enough about him that people will be interested in reading it. I know Vince will probably be pissed that it's not the scandalous article or exposé he was really hoping for, but it'll be about Jack, and it will bring positive press to the paper and a local high school. He can't argue with that kind of good press.

At least that's what I'm hoping.

I'm just finishing the update to my notes when my cell phone rings, and Gina's name pops up on the caller ID.

I answer immediately. "Hey, Gina, what's up?"

"Hey, girl, I was wondering what you were up to for the next couple of days and if you're down for some girl time?"

"Um, yes! I miss you. I'd love to see you. How soon can you be here?"

"Funny you should ask." She laughs. "I'm only about an hour away. I took a risk that you'd say yes and just got in my car this morning. I'm desperate to get out of San Fran. Collin keeps trying to convince me to give him another chance and won't leave me alone, so I thought I'd come visit you for a few days and get away from his annoying, cheating ass. Plus my mom has been hounding me to come visit her, and Long Beach isn't too far from you, so I figure this kills two birds with one stone."

"Absolutely. You know you're always welcome. I'm just at the paper finishing up some work, but I could meet you at my place as soon as you get into town."

"Sounds great. I'll give you a call when I'm a few minutes away."

"Okay," I respond happily. "Talk to you then."

I hang up quickly, excited to see my best friend after a month apart and anxious to finish my work so I can get out of here. It's only after another minute of thinking of what we should get for dinner tonight that I remember I already have plans with Jack. I quickly text him.

Me: Hey! Gina just called me to let me know she's on her way for a surprise visit. I'm so sorry, but I'm going to have to cancel our dinner plans tonight.

He responds almost immediately.

Jack: Cool that she's coming for a visit, but I hate that I won't get to see you. Do you think she'd be down for dinner if she wasn't the third wheel? I'd love to meet her. I could bring Max. Thoughts?

Me: Let me check with Gina.

I quickly call Gina back and fill her in on Jack's offer.

"That actually sounds like a fabulous idea since I really want to meet your guy. Also, gives me a chance to make sure he's got good intentions this time. And if not, I've been practicing my kickboxing..."

I laugh at her protectiveness and tell her I'll let him know and see her later. I text Jack back to let him know we're a go for dinner.

Gina arrives not too long after and we both squeal and hug each other like it's been years instead of a little over a month since we've seen each other. I know it's so cliché for women to do that with their girlfriends, but honestly, I couldn't stop it even if I tried. Frankly, it's the one moment where I feel like I can relate to the excitement dogs must feel when their owners come home.

We both change into clothes that are slightly dressier than our business and travel wear. I'm catching her up on everything that's been going on when I hear the buzzer to my building. We grab our purses and head down to meet Jack. When he comes into view, I'm surprised to see Will Edmonson standing with him instead of Max.

"Good Lord, who is that handsome hunk of a man next to your guy?" Gina asks quietly.

I laughingly reply, "That would be Will. He plays for the Wolves with Jack."

"My God, it should be illegal for a man to be that attractive."

I catch Gina's blush and can't help smirking. My friend is not one who is easily overwhelmed by a handsome man. She's usually feisty and confident. Very little causes her to blush or become shy, but here she is, looking almost overwhelmed with bashfulness.

I'm further intrigued when we greet the guys and I notice Will appreciatively check her out. When I catch the slight blush on his cheeks as they shake hands, I decide that I'm going to have to talk to Jack about Will and find out as much as I can about him. He's always seemed like a good guy, fairly quiet and reserved, but Gina deserves the best. I'm not going to encourage this if Will turns out to be a player like most football guys. She's had enough of asshole boyfriends.

At dinner, their mutual attraction is even more obvious. Will occasionally becomes more reserved and almost withdrawn before Gina inevitably pulls him back into the fold and he's blushing like a schoolgirl all over again. Gina seems to have found her footing, although I notice she's being subtly flirty instead of outrightly so.

I make eyes at Jack—*are you seeing this?* He gives me a brief nod but seems surprised and a little cautious about it. Why would he be surprised? Gina is amazing. Will would be lucky to have her.

We go out for drinks after dinner and stay out much later than we probably should seeing as how the guys have a game tomorrow. When they drop us off, I ask Jack to call me after he gets home. He kisses me sweetly and then it's just us girls.

"So..." I start, "Will seems pretty great, huh?"

Gina laughs. "Oh my God, was I too obvious? At first, I

thought maybe he'd just be smoking hot and a total dummy, like some athletes. Or a complete bore who's obsessed with himself. But he was kind and thoughtful. I can't believe how easy the conversation was all night! And, by the way, Jack is awesome. I'm so glad things are working out with you two. You guys are so clearly meant to be together, it's almost sickening."

I laugh and shrug my shoulders at that comment, but I can't help but feel giddy at the idea that someone else sees how perfect we are together. I was so reluctant at first but having Gina's approval makes me feel more confident in my decision to give him another chance.

"I'll get the dirt on Will for you, if you want."

Gina sighs. "I would love that, but seriously, what's the point? I live in the Bay Area and he lives here. It's not like anything could ever happen. I'm just going to soak in the bliss of having an incredible night with my best friend and meeting a guy who makes me believe there are still good ones out there. And on that note, I'm gonna head to bed. I'm exhausted from driving all day. I love ya. I'll see you in the morning."

"Get some rest. We'll have a beach day tomorrow before the game since I took the day off."

"Sounds heavenly. Night."

I leave her and go into my own room. It's not long before I hear her snoring softly on the couch. Gina is not typically a snorer. The few times I've experienced it, we'd either been shamefully wasted or exhausted beyond belief, so I know she's down for the count. That's why I don't bother whispering when Jack calls.

I cut to the chase. "So tell me about Will."

He sighs heavily into the phone. "Honestly, I was pretty surprised about tonight. I've

never seen him act like that. Babe, I'm not sure you should

encourage anything between him and Gina if that's what you're thinking."

"I'm not, but only because Gina said there's no point in getting too excited since they live so far apart. But why are you saying that? Is he a bad guy?"

"Not even a little bit. He's one of the best guys I know, but he hasn't had an easy time for quite a while."

"What do you mean?"

He sighs heavily again, and I can tell he's debating on whether he should tell me or not. My journalist curiosity is piqued, so I let the silence fill the line between us. Eventually, my patience is rewarded.

"Okay, I'll tell you his story, but don't tell Gina. It's really not my story to tell, and I barely feel comfortable telling you, but I feel like it's the only way you'll understand."

"Okay."

"Will was engaged."

"What happened? Did she cheat on him or something?"

"She died."

I'm shocked back against my pillow. "What?" I can barely whisper the word, but Jack

hears me.

"Yeah. It was about a year ago. I think the anniversary just passed actually. It was a drunk driver. I don't know all the details, but I've always suspected they had just had a fight, based on some comments he's made. He was a wreck when she died and has been completely emotionally cut off ever since. He doesn't date at all. As far as I know, he hasn't even looked at another woman. I don't want to see your friend get hurt, and I just don't think he's in the right mindset for a relationship yet."

I was not expecting that to be the reason Gina and Will wouldn't work out. I can't help but feel heartbroken for Will. He's such a nice guy. He definitely didn't deserve something so awful to happen to him. I'm surprised I never heard anything in the news about it. You'd think that would be a pretty big deal, but I guess he has one hell of a publicist if it never hit the papers.

"Thank you for telling me. I won't tell Gina, but you're right. It does help me understand why he's probably not good for Gina right now."

"Yeah, I wish things were different. It did seem like they hit it off pretty well. There was definitely some chemistry there, but I doubt Will is going to let himself go there with her."

We talk for a few more minutes before saying goodnight. As I start to drift off to sleep, I wish Will and Gina had met at a different time. I can't help thinking that they'd still be perfect together.

THIRTY-TWO

Jack

Football has been my sole focus for so long that it never bothered me how much of my time it consumes during the season, but I'm feeling the strain of that now. It's been a whole week since I've been able to see Paige, and I'm dying to see her again, to see her gorgeous smile and the way her eyes practically dazzle when she looks at me. For the first time in nearly ten years, football isn't my priority. She is.

After practice, I drive over to Paige's apartment to pick her up for a big football party tonight at a local club. She texted me earlier, letting me know that Gina was able to drive down again for the weekend. I thought it might be nice for Paige to have another friendly face since these events tend to get a little overwhelming.

Plus, I'm a little curious to see how Will is going to respond to being in the same room with Gina again.

As soon as I see Paige, I finally feel whole for the first time in a week.

"Hey," she greets me.

"Hey, gorgeous," I say as I lean down to kiss her sweet, pink lips. I kiss her hair before letting her go in order to greet Gina, who is standing behind her.

"Hey, Gina."

"Hey, Jack. Thanks for the invite to this party tonight. I haven't been out dancing in forever."

"Anytime. You ladies ready to go?"

"Yep," Paige says, grabbing her clutch and opening the front door.

The club is already hopping by the time we arrive. The whole team was invited as well as donors, sponsors, and celebrities. I usually have to attend at least one big event like this each season, but this is the first time in a long time that I've actually looked forward to it. I'm excited to have Paige by my side. It feels like we're a team, and that energizes me in a way that nothing has before.

I look around the club and notice they seemed to have let in a lot of ladies, which isn't uncommon when it's a full-team event, especially given how many of our players are single. Unfortunately, most of the women that come to events like these are jersey chasers, which has never been my thing. They're way too unpredictable.

I pull Paige closer to my side, even more thankful that she's here. I have a trustworthy partner by my side and not just someone who wants me for fifteen minutes of fame or to rub elbows with the rich and famous of LA.

Gina suggests we get drinks, so we all walk over to the bar. Paige orders a vodka cranberry, while Gina orders a gin and tonic. I stick with my usual whiskey on the rocks. The bartender hands us our drinks just as Max saunters over, his eyes glued to Gina.

"Well, who do we have here?" He asks as he slides his eyes down Gina's curvy frame. I'm about to tell him to chill when Gina sticks her hand out to him.

"Gina Rodrigo, Paige's best friend." She looks him up and down as his hand wraps around hers. "And you are?"

He smirks. "Max Donnelly. Jack's best friend." His face twists slightly in a grimace before he pulls his hand away, shaking it out. "You've got one hell of a grip."

There's just a hint of lasciviousness in his tone, but Gina definitely picks up on it. Her smile turns predatory as she takes a step closer to him. "Just a word of advice, Max." She leans up in an attempt to whisper closer to his ear, although he still has several inches on her, his six-foot, one-inch frame no match for her much shorter one. "Don't eye fuck a woman until you know exactly who she is."

Max's eyes shoot straight to me, his eyebrows rising in surprise. He lets out a shocked laugh before looking back at Gina with admiration shining in his eyes. "Damn, girl. This whole strong, sexy woman thing you've got going on is really doing it for me." His shock morphs into a joyfully excited smile.

Gina steps away from him, shaking her head. She turns to me. "This one is trouble, isn't he?"

I nod. "The worst kind."

Max lightly punches my arm. "Dude, come on, you're supposed to be my wingman, not a cock block."

Gina smiles. "Don't worry, sweetie. Your cock never stood a chance with me anyway."

Paige snorts into her drink, finally failing at holding back her laughter. Gina turns to her, and the second they make eye contact, both ladies burst out laughing. Max and I look at each other.

"Did I miss something?" he asks me.

"If you did, then so did I." I shrug and look around, my gaze landing on a familiar face. Will Edmonson is sitting farther down the bar, glaring at something behind me. I turn around and see Max has sidled back up to Gina. He says something that makes her throw her head back, letting out a laugh, while her hand rests on his arm. His expression is bright with happiness at seeing her reaction.

When I turn back to Will, his glare has deepened. He tosses back his drink and then makes his way over to us.

Well, damn, this should be interesting.

THIRTY-THREE

Paige

Gina and Max laugh easily with each other and I shake my head at Gina's ability to make friends wherever she goes. She has a gift. People are naturally drawn to her. It's just frustrating that she hasn't been able to find a guy who values her the way she deserves.

I turn to look at Jack to get his take on our friends' flirty banter and notice his attention is elsewhere. I follow his gaze and see Will walking toward us, his expression stoic but also slightly pissed off. As he gets closer, his body seems to be vibrating with frustration.

As if Gina can sense a change in the energy around us, her eyes turn straight to Will, while Max continues talking. I look back and forth between Gina and Will as if I'm watching a tennis match. Their gazes stay locked on each other, and I swear you could cut the sexual tension with a knife.

Oh yeah, there is definitely something between these two.

I smile and sip my drink, wishing I had some popcorn so I could thoroughly enjoy the show in front of me. I look at Jack and see him shooting glances between the two like he's trying to work out what's going on here.

Finally, his eyes land on mine, and I arch my brow, shooting him a look that says *I told you there was something between them*. He reads my expression accurately, a small smile gracing his full lips, and shakes his head.

Max finally picks up on the fact that he's completely lost Gina's attention and looks between her and Will, his shoulders dropping slightly before his look turns calculated. He glances at the two of them again before stepping closer to Gina and sliding an arm around her shoulders. If he notices her body stiffen, he doesn't let on.

I watch, enraptured by the display in front of me. Things just got even more interesting. I mean, hell, at this rate, these guys are going to have to whip 'em out and measure them right here if the macho display that's starting is any indication of what's to come.

Will's gaze turns dark as he eyes Max's arm draped around Gina's shoulders, holding her close to his body. Gina's cautious gaze never strays from Will.

"Hey, man. How's it going?" Max asks Will casually.

Will's jaw clenches.

I'm on the edge of my seat, waiting to see how he reacts.

Come on, Will, fight for her. You know you want to.

Will looks at Gina closely and his mouth opens, but no words come out. He briefly glances down to the floor, but it appears that's all he needs to fortify his usual expression of casual indifference. When he looks back up, his typical mask is firmly in place. Finally, he answers Max's question. "It's going. Mind if I join y'all?"

My ears perk up at the slight southern accent that I've never heard from him before. Huh, I wonder where that came from.

He clears his throat, and when he speaks again, there's no hint of an accent. "Nice to see you again, Gina."

My journalistic instincts have reared their head, and now

I'm more curious about Will than ever. Especially if he ends up being interested in Gina, although the jury's still out on that one. He's so hot and cold. I was convinced when he walked over here that he was going to make a move on her so Max would back off, but now he's back to acting casually indifferent.

"Good to see you too, Will," Gina responds with a soft smile. Her eyes rove over Will, and I can't help but notice this is a very different reaction than the playfulness she threw Max's way. I know Gina well enough to recognize that she genuinely likes Will.

Max watches Will closely as he asks, "So, Gina, you got a boyfriend back in San Francisco?"

If looks could kill, Max would be dead right now from Will's stare. I have to fight back an awkward laugh as I watch Max fuck with Will. It's clearly working, and Max knows it as Will's faked indifference immediately disappears. Max smiles wide, watching Will's jaw clench and his fingers grip the beer in his hand until they turn white. I'm honestly a little worried he might break the glass.

Gina looks between the two guys and picks up on what Max is doing. She probably would've caught on to it a lot sooner if she wasn't distracted by her own response to Will.

She turns to Max, a playful smirk on her face. "Actually, no. I've yet to find someone man enough to handle me." She winks at him just as he's about to take a drink and adds, "Do you know anybody?"

Max chokes on his drink, his eyes going wide as he looks at her. Her smile is sweet, but her eyes are teasing. "I know what you're doing," she says quietly enough that only Max and I probably heard her.

He shoots her an innocent expression. "Who, me? I'm not doing anything but trying to enjoy the company of a beautiful woman."

Max is really starting to remind me of Eddie Haskell from *Leave it to Beaver*. I bet he's used to talking his way out of anything, but he's clearly met his match with Gina. I glance at Will, who's watching them closely, and I decide to give everyone a break from this standoff.

"Gina, I need to use the ladies' room. Come with me?"

She quickly tosses back the last little bit of her drink and then slides her arm through mine. "Gentlemen, don't kill each other before we get back."

As soon as we get into the bathroom, Gina walks straight to the sink, bracing herself against the bright white ceramic.

"Thanks for the save out there."

"Anytime. That's what friends are for. I could tell you were ready for a break from all that testosterone," I reply.

She turns to me, resting her hip against the sink and crossing her arms. "What was that out there anyway?"

"Beats me. I can't tell if Max is genuinely interested in you or if he was just trying to fuck with Will." I lean my head side to side, replaying the whole scene. "Honestly, I think he was trying to get to Will."

"Why would he do that?"

"I'm not sure." I wonder if it has to do with Will's obvious reaction to Gina. Jack said that Will hasn't been interested in dating since his fiancée died. Max must know that too. Unfortunately, I promised Jack I wouldn't tell Gina about Will's past. Maybe I can tell her some things.

"I think it's been a long time since Will dated. Maybe they're just trying to get more of a reaction out of him, or simply messing with him because they're getting a reaction at all."

Gina looks off at nothing. "Yeah, I suppose. Do you really think Will was reacting, though? He seemed more annoyed."

"I definitely thought he was reacting."

She shrugs. "I don't know. He's so hard to read sometimes.

He's so hot and cold," she voices out loud my thought from earlier. "When we had that dinner with the four of us, he'd have moments where he pulled away. Then, he'd be warm and flirty. It's so confusing."

I'm about to speak when she straightens, turns to the mirror, and slides her hands through her hair, fixing the few flyaways present. "You know, it doesn't matter. I live in San Francisco and he lives in LA. I don't know why I'm even worrying about this. It's not like we're ever going to be a thing anyway."

With that, she turns back to me, standing tall with her shoulders back. "You ready to go back out there?" We've barely been gone five minutes, but I can tell by her stance and determined expression that she's ready to get back out there and prove she's not affected by him.

She's doing her tough girl thing. It's something I've noticed she does a lot more since her ex cheated on her. It's her armor—her way of protecting herself—so I'm not going to push her.

Not yet, anyway.

THIRTY-FOUR

Jack

Paige and Gina have hardly been gone two minutes when Will finally breaks the silent standoff he's been having with Max ever since they went to the bathroom.

He steps up to Max, an intimidating glare on his face. "Leave Gina alone. She's a nice girl. She doesn't deserve a guy who can't commit."

What's funny about that comment is that he has no idea Max has barely been with any woman since he first laid eyes on Cassie Jones, who works in the LA Wolves business office. He may be an unrepentant flirt and play up the single guy attitude, but that's not who he really is.

Will has a few inches on Max, but that doesn't stop Max from going toe to toe with him. "Are you talking about me...or you?"

I grab Will's arm as I see it move, stopping him from reaching out to grab Max. "Fuck you, Donnelly," he spits out. They stare at each other, not saying a word, aggression building between them.

Finally, Max shakes his head and smiles at Will, breaking the tension. "Dude, seriously, if you like her, you don't have to go all caveman. Just tell me and I'll back off. I'm just fucking with you anyway. Gina is Paige's best friend. She's too close to home, so she's all yours."

"I don't want her like that," he growls out.

I hear a gasp right behind me and turn to see Paige shooting daggers at Will, while Gina's face fills with hurt. Her expression changes quickly to indifference, and if I hadn't been looking right at her, I would've missed the pain on her face.

Paige turns and speaks to me, her voice noticeably colder. "Sorry to interrupt. I just wanted to let you know that Gina and I are going to dance for a bit. I didn't want you to worry." I can tell by her tone that she's fighting her anger at Will.

"Okay. I'll come join you once I finish my drink."

She nods before leaving a brief kiss on my lips. She grabs Gina's hand, and they walk away, already swaying to the beat of the music.

I turn back to see regret written all over Will's face. "You don't think she heard that, do you?"

"Paige definitely did, so I'm pretty sure Gina did too."

"Fuck," he mutters as he slides his hand through his hair and looks out at the dance floor.

I watch my friend closely and think back to my conversation with Paige after our double date. She thought there was something between him and Gina, and now I'm convinced she's right. I just really hope he stops fighting it before he loses his chance.

Matt Fischer, another player on my team, stumbles over to our group. He pats me on the back, and I notice that he reeks of beer. "Jack! How ya doin', buddy? I didn't know you were here!"

"It's a wonder you were even able to walk over here," Will observes.

I take in his disheveled appearance and the red lipstick stains on his neck. Matt is one hell of a tight end, but off the field, he's a bit of a disaster. He's the biggest playboy I've ever met, and that's really saying something in this profession.

He stumbles toward the bar that Max is now casually leaning against. "Barkeep," he shouts. "Another round for me and my buddies!" He circles his finger around and then slaps his hand on the bar. Max rolls his eyes and turns, leaning toward the bartender.

"Bring him a water."

The bartender nods and goes about making our drinks. Will and I move forward, Will positioning himself on the right of Matt, Max on his left, and me in the middle. Matt definitely needs to sober up a bit, or he's going to regret this in the morning.

I help Matt sit on the stool in front of the bar and watch him slump down with his head resting on his hand while his elbow rests on the bar top. Max shakes his head at the sight before us and then redirects his attention to me.

"It seems like things are going well with Paige."

I glance behind me and find her out on the dance floor, laughing with Gina and looking sexy as hell. I turn back to Max and nod. "Things are better than I ever imagined. There have been a couple of bumps, but it really feels like the past nine years apart didn't happen."

"Nine years?!" Matt blurts out. "Fuck, dude, you've been pining over that woman for nine years?"

I observe Matt cautiously. He and I aren't particularly close. We never really hang out outside of practices and games. I'm just about to suggest that we switch topics when Max speaks first.

Shaking his head at Matt, he says, "Ignore him, Jack. He's drunk as fuck. He's not even going to remember this conversation in the morning."

"Yeah, I suppose you're right."

"So, has the reporter thing come back up?" Max asks.

"Not really. Things have been good, and I don't think she'd sabotage us like that.

Actually, things have been better than good." I try to find the words to describe how I'm feeling. I'm not used to sharing my emotions with the guys, especially not in a nightclub in Hollywood. "I didn't think I'd get to be with her like this again."

"You mean sex," Matt nods knowingly, practically shouting his words.

I roll my eyes at him. "Matt, you're fucking drunk, dude. Here, drink this water." I grab the glass from the bar and hand it to him. He's definitely going to feel this in the morning.

I turn my focus back to Max and Will. "Everything is different with Paige. I'm different with her." I tell them about our date at Point Fermin Lighthouse and how things have changed since that night. I trust her more than I've ever trusted anyone, which might be stupid given her profession, but I'm going with my gut on this one, even if that small kernel of doubt is still buried deep.

I glance at the dance floor where Paige is dancing with Gina. I ache to hold her and feel the connection that's always there when we touch. I need her to soothe this fear that lives deep in me. To show me that those doubts are just stupid insecurities from past mistakes and not something I ever have to worry about with her.

"I'm gonna go dance with my girl." I nod to the guys and leave them to watch over Matt.

The second I slide my hands around Paige's waist, she leans back into me, her body loose and relaxed. I breathe in her warm sweet fragrance, and the strain in my body dissipates.

I draw circles around the skin on her shoulder and watch in fascination as goosebumps break out across her arm. I lightly tug on her ear with my teeth, and the gasp of pleasure from her makes me instantly hard.

We dance for a little longer before I can't take any more without wanting to ravish her right here.

We make our exit only after Max promises to drop Gina off at her parents' place in Long Beach where she was planning to stay so she could spend the morning with them before heading back to the Bay Area.

When we get back to my place, I gently lay Paige on the couch and slide my body down hers, kissing every exposed inch of skin I can find. It doesn't take us long to shed our clothes and connect in the way we know best. As I move within her, I'm convinced that her body was made for mine.

Sometime in the middle of the night I wake her again with my head between her legs. She comes gloriously hard, her thighs gripping my face and practically suffocating me.

Not a bad way to go.

When the tremors finally still and her legs fall from my cheeks, I move my body up and kiss her lovingly. She smiles at me and then pushes me over and straddles my body.

"Your turn," she whispers.

I move my hands through her gorgeous brown locks as she kisses her way down my body. My breath hitches in my chest as she starts by teasing me with her tongue before taking my entire length.

"Fuck, that feels amazing." I can barely restrain myself from coming, she's got me so worked up. She is dangerously good at this.

Jesus Christ, I'm going to come.

It only takes her a couple more hard sucks of my steel erection before I'm right at the edge. "Paige..." I take a deep breath, trying to delay my release. "Fuck, babe, I'm about to come."

She hums against my cock, and it's my undoing. I come hard

with a throaty groan, and she takes it all. She kisses her way back up my body as I come down from my intense release.

I love you.

The words are damn near ripped out of my mouth when I look in her eyes. I recognize that look. She loves me too.

I kiss her fiercely while we use our bodies to speak the words neither of us are yet able to, and when we come together, all we see is each other. I fall asleep with Paige's head resting on my shoulder, her arm across my stomach and my fingers twirled in her hair.

We're going to make it this time is my last thought before sleep overcomes me.

THIRTY-FIVE

Paige

I walk into the office, a woman on a mission. This past weekend with Jack was so perfect. I've thought endlessly about this article assignment, and I need to be upfront with Vince that I will not be writing the exposé he's hoping for. I'm sick of lying to Jack, even if it's mostly only a lie of omission at this point.

I don't want this article between us anymore, especially after the past couple of days. I love him with every ounce of my being, and I'm not willing to risk the happiness we've found, not even for my dream job.

I knock on Vince's door. "You got a second?"

He briefly glances up from his computer. "Actually, I'm glad you stopped by. Where are you at with the Fuller story?"

"About that..." I take a breath, prepared to list all the reasons I memorized on my way into work this morning when he cuts me off.

"Let me stop you. I'll rephrase. You have one week to get me a completed story, or I'll have no choice but to terminate your position with this paper."

My jaw drops. "What?! On what grounds?"

His look couldn't be any more condescending if he tried.

"Paige, you know I only hired

you for this. I won't deny that your writing is strong, and the smaller pieces you've worked on in the time you've been here have been good. That being said, I can find hundreds of journalists to write me strong articles. None have the in that you do with Jack. I know you've been seeing him. TMZ was more than happy to break the story that he's dating a reporter."

I blanch at his comment. I knew TMZ had written something brief about us, but we've kept our relationship relatively private, and that article came out over a week ago. Vince never mentioned it, so I assumed he hadn't seen it. I'm embarrassed because I should've known better. Journalists always keep up with the news.

"I am dating Jack, but that's why I can't write this article. It's a serious conflict of interest."

He leans across his desk. "Paige, I don't give a shit about your relationship. I want the article. Write it, or you're fired. We're done here. You can see yourself out." He turns back to his computer, dismissing me.

"You can't just fire me because I won't write this article about Jack."

"California is an at-will state, which means I don't need a reason to fire you."

I look at him carefully, my heart beating furiously in my chest. "Yes, but it's illegal to fire me in retaliation for not writing what you want me to."

Vince's expression is snide when he asks, "And how are you going to prove that's the reason you were terminated?"

I clench my jaw and fight my reaction to lash out at Vince.

He nods his head once, knowing I don't have a leg to stand on. "Now, I suggest you get writing if you value your career. I can promise you, Paige, I will ruin you in this industry before you even reach the door if you don't give me what I want."

Without speaking, I stand up on shaky legs and walk out. I look around at the desks, some with reporters, some empty because people are out working on their stories. I start heading to my desk, but when I see Alicia hovering nearby I quickly change directions and head for the breakroom. She talks to me whenever we're in the same vicinity, and I just can't deal with that today. I need caffeine and a moment to take a breath and think this through. I've never felt so completely defeated about my job before.

I enter the breakroom, grab a Coke from the fridge, and sit at the table. This is my dream job. Paper journalism is a dying art, and there are a ton of people in line to work at a major paper like the *Chronicle*. Vince is right; I'd be easy to replace.

My heart sinks. I'm actually going to have to choose between Jack and my career. A tear slips down my cheek at the thought. When I hear a throat clearing, I quickly swipe it away and look up to the entrance of the breakroom, nervous that Alicia saw me duck in here.

But it's not Alicia standing at the entrance. A woman, who looks to be in her early forties, stands just inside the door. She looks at me with a kindness that almost breaks down the wall I just barely finished building. She's dressed in a beautiful, perfectly tailored, royal-purple dress. It's one of those dresses that screams sophistication and professionalism. This woman exudes power and clearly comes from wealth. She radiates confidence, and I've never been so jealous of a stranger as I am of her in this moment. I could use some confidence right about now.

"You okay?" she asks.

I look down at my Coke briefly in an attempt to find some composure before I glance back at her. "I'm fine."

"Bullshit."

My eyes widen at hearing a curse from this refined woman. I was not expecting that.

She explains, "No one is ever 'fine,' and if they say they are, they're full of shit. The world would be a lot better off if people were honest about how they were feeling instead of just saying they're 'good' or 'fine.' So, I'm going to ask again, and you're going to give me an honest answer this time. Are you okay?"

I shake my head. I know it's probably a terrible idea to trust this woman. I don't know who she is, but I'm crumbling, and I've never been so unsure of my footing before. Maybe she'll be able to give me some good advice.

I find my voice, "No, I'm not."

She sits down at the table next to me. "Want to talk about it?"

"It's a complicated story." Hah! Understatement.

"My favorite kind."

I smile at her. "This is my dream job. But I was given an assignment that I don't think I

can complete."

I hesitate, unsure if I should really unload information on this woman. After all, she's in a newspaper office. She could be a journalist herself. Although I get the vibe that she's much more than that. Call it a reporter's instinct.

"Go on," she encourages.

"I'm supposed to write a story, but I fell in love with the subject of the article. He and I have a history, and I guess the feelings were still there. I...I can't write this story, but if I don't, I lose the career I've worked my ass off for."

"In my experience, men have never been worth the risk. Men come and go, darling, but typically the dream job only comes around once."

I let her words marinate in my head, merging with a thought that I've had floating around for a few weeks.

"What if your dream changes?"

"Hmm." She seems to genuinely ponder my question. "I've always been a firm believer that your career is your legacy. Your dreams drive you to build that career to its highest potential. But I suppose for everyone it's different. Some women dream of having a family and staying home with their kids, and others dream of becoming the next Ruth Bader Ginsburg. At the end of the day, the only thing that matters is that you've followed your dream and not someone else's, even if your dream has changed along the way." She leans in. "And perhaps there are other opportunities out there that may be better suited to your new dream."

I absorb her words and process them silently. She excuses herself, leaving me her business card if I want to talk anymore. Without looking at it, I nod a goodbye before getting lost in my thoughts again.

I think back to my sixteen-year-old self and how in love with Jack I was then. Since I was a girl, Jack has been my dream. I always thought we'd have a life together. When that fell apart, I threw myself into different activities. My career became my focus, but now that he's back in the picture, I can't help but feel like my dream is shifting back to that one I had all those years ago.

I'm stronger with Jack. He makes me feel like I can do anything. I don't think I'd actually miss this particular job. It hasn't exactly turned out to be what I thought it would, and I certainly wouldn't miss Vince being an ass. Yet, it hurts to breathe just thinking of the possibility of losing Jack again.

I realize what I have to do. I head back to my desk and instantly start brainstorming my article changes. The words begin to flow out of me. This article will make my feelings clear to Vince and Jack.

And then I can focus on my new dream.

THIRTY-SIX

Jack

I've only gotten to see Paige a few times this week due to an article she's been working on and a lot of promotional work I've been doing. I have a couple of days off and convinced Paige to take a few days off so that we can get away together.

I pick her up Thursday morning and drive us out to Malibu. Max's dad has a house on a private beach that he hardly ever uses, and when Max offered it for a getaway, I snatched it up. I have to be back Sunday in order to be rested and ready for our Monday night game, but this gives us a couple of days away from everything.

The drive is long, but when we arrive at the house—okay, let's be real, it's a fucking mansion—it's all worth it.

"Holy shit. This place is gorgeous." She took the words right out of my mouth.

"Fuck, Max definitely downplayed this place."

We walk in the house and take in the modern extravagance coating every inch. I've been in a lot of fancy mansions, but this one is a step above. The house is over ten thousand square feet and has three floors, twelve bedrooms, fourteen bathrooms, a movie theater, gym, tennis court, infinity pool, and private beach access. The kitchen is a chef's wet dream.

We turn off our phones—our deal while we're away so we can focus on this time together instead of getting distracted by the outside world—then we go to look around. It takes us over an hour to fully explore the whole property.

We make a quick lunch in the fully stocked kitchen that Max left for us and then we head down to the private beach. The weather is perfect at almost seventy degrees and sunny, with only the slightest breeze.

Paige looks at me saucily. "Think you could do me a favor?" she asks, shaking a bottle of sunscreen.

I give her my most seductive smile. "Oh, most definitely, gorgeous."

I may or may not take an exorbitant and unnecessary amount of time rubbing sunscreen all over every exposed inch of Paige's delicious body. She doesn't complain. By the time I'm done, I'm rock hard, but determined to spend quality time with her, not naked. I know, it's crazy, but I also don't want her to think we're only about sex.

We spend the rest of the afternoon lazing around the beach. Eventually, we decide we're both hungry again. I fire up the grill, while Paige grabs us some beers. I'm laughing at the story Paige just finished about her and Gina in college when she surprises me by asking about the future.

"Where do you see yourself in five years?"

With you.

I hesitate. I want to be honest, but this is the first time we've really talked about the future. We've spent a lot of time updating each other on our pasts and presents, but not the future. Is it too soon to lay my cards on the table?

I turn to her and see her looking at me expectantly and

almost hopefully. That's all I need to make my decision. "I see myself with you."

I wish I could take a picture of the smile that breaks out on her face. It makes me feel like the king of the fucking world.

"You do?"

I nod my head. "How about you? Where do you see yourself in five years?"

Paige never breaks eye contact. "With you," she says strongly.

I set my beer down and walk over to her. She follows me with her eyes as I lean down, placing my hands on the arms of the chair she's sitting on and trapping her body with mine. "You want to be my future?"

"I want to be your everything," she whispers.

I kiss her deeply, pulling her up from the chair and holding her body as close to me as possible. She pulls away, giggling and looking over my shoulder. "Jack, the burgers."

I turn around. "Oh shit!"

I release her with one more quick kiss and run back over to the grill, flipping the burgers that are now slightly charred on one side. I let the conversation go and we discuss lighter topics while we eat.

It isn't until after dinner, when I'm buried deep inside of her that I bring us back to that conversation. I thrust gently, her body arching underneath mine in pleasure. I can tell my pace is driving her crazy with need. It's doing the same to me, but I know the wait will be worth it in the end.

"You want to be my everything, Paige?"

Her eyes are hazy with lust and something else that she hasn't said since we were seventeen.

"Yes," she whispers.

I kiss her, letting all my emotions flow between us. "You already are," I whisper back.

Tears form at the corner of her eyes, and I'm about to panic that I messed this up when she speaks the words I've been dying to hear. "I love you, Jack."

For the first time in nearly a decade, my heart skips in my chest. "I love you, too, Paige."

She leans up to kiss me, and our mouths fuse together with need, want, and so much more love than I ever knew was possible. We continue to whisper those three words over and over while we make love.

THIRTY-SEVEN

Paige

"Oh my God, yes!" I scream, coming so hard I swear I see stars. I used to be envious of people who had marathon sex, and now I'm one of them.

Since our declarations of love last night, Jack and I have only left the bed to use the bathroom or get sustenance. Other than that, we've been ravaging each other over and over, snuggling naked between bouts of sex. It has been absolutely fan-fucking-tastic.

"I think I've officially lost track of how many orgasms I've had since we got here," I huff out, trying to catch my breath.

Jack, who is annoyingly, yet divinely athletic and in insane physical shape, merely grunts as he splays out next to me, recovering from his own release. I think I've finally tested the limits of his athleticism.

"Okay..." Jack takes a couple of deep breaths and then turns to me with an enigmatic smile spreading across his face. "I think I might actually need to take a break from sex."

He suddenly looks horrified. "I can't believe I just said that," he whispers.

I burst out in a fit of laughter but nod my head in agreement. My body is completely spent.

I practically drool as I watch him roll out of bed and walk to the bathroom, completely comfortable with his nakedness. God, those abs, and arms, and that delicious looking ass. Ugh, why is he so sexy?!

I can't believe this man is mine.

I smile in sheer bliss as I replay our declarations of love throughout the night. I feel more complete than I have in a long time. I turn my head toward the bathroom to see Jack standing in the doorway, smirking at me.

"What?" I ask.

He shakes his head, looking down at the floor to hide his smile, and then walks toward me. He cups my face with his large, calloused hands and kisses me reverently. I've never felt more cherished in my entire life.

"I love you so much," he whispers.

"I love you too, so, so much," I whisper back.

I'm suddenly overcome with emotion and can't stop the tear from escaping my eye. Jack

sees it immediately, and I hate the frown that mars his face.

"What's wrong?"

I shake my head. "Nothing."

He looks at me doubtfully. "I'm serious, Jack. Nothing is wrong. I'm crying because I'm so ridiculously happy."

He wipes the next couple of tears gently from my face with his thumb, looking at them uncertainly.

"Jack, I haven't been this happy and content since we were sixteen. Since before my family moved us to Chicago."

"Me either," he admits.

"When you broke up with me, I was so devastated."

"Paige..." his voice breaks, and the pain I felt all those years ago is clear on his face. He felt it too.

"I survived, but I was never the same."

"I know the feeling," he whispers.

"This is the first time in nearly ten years that I've felt whole. When we first broke up, I tried so hard to get over it. People kept telling me it was just young love and that I'd find something deeper as I got older. Yet, no one ever came close to making me feel the way you do. Not once. Not until you kissed me again for the first time. And then that feeling came back."

"I know exactly what you're talking about."

"You do?"

He looks at me. "Paige, I broke my own heart just as much as yours when I ended things

after you moved. I'd never felt that way about anyone, and I've never felt that way about anyone since. I've wondered a million times what would've happened if I hadn't given up on us and just fought through the distance.

"There were so many times I almost called you because life sucked without you. Paige, you weren't just the love of my life. You were my best friend, my everything. I threw myself into football after we broke up because I could barely stand to be alone with my thoughts, and football was a great distraction."

"It worked out for you; you were meant to be a football player. You're incredible out there."

He kisses my hand. "I appreciate that, babe, but it doesn't change the fact that it sucked for me too. I've been missing something ever since I let you go. I'm just relieved to know you feel this too."

"I do."

"God, I can't wait to hear you say that in a different circumstance." He grins playfully with me, but my heart starts fluttering crazily in my chest.

"Are you saying what I think you're saying?" I laugh with nervous excitement.

"Too soon?"

"Maybe just a bit. We've only been back together for a couple of months."

"As far as I'm concerned, I'd marry you tomorrow. But, now that I think about it more, you're probably right. When I propose, I want you to be completely swept off your feet." He smiles brightly.

I kiss him, and it's not long before we're eagerly enjoying each other's bodies all over again, forgetting all about our earlier exhaustion.

After a blissful three days at our Malibu hideaway, we're back on the PCH driving home. Jack teases me about my love of romance novels, something he apparently never knew about me. I slap him on the arm, laughing at his endless ribbing. He rubs his arm and pretends to be hurt.

I roll my eyes. "Oh, come on, I didn't hit you that hard."

His frown immediately transforms into a radiant grin. "No, you didn't. I'm made of stronger stuff than that. Besides, I always loved it when you'd slap my arm. It's like being hit by a pixie." He winks at me before turning his attention back to the road.

"I do not hit like a pixie!"

I'm not really offended. We've always been this playful with each other, and it takes me back to when we were best friends, long before we ever started dating. The familiarity is comforting.

He takes my hand, brings it to his lips, and kisses it sweetly. I melt at the sudden sweetness, and our conversation fades into a companionable silence.

The drive is much shorter coming home than it was driving to Malibu. Traffic is on our side today, unfortunately. I'd love to continue to drag out my time with Jack. These past few days have been absolute heaven. Waking up with him holding me close and sharing simple tasks, like making a meal together, has been everything I ever dreamed of.

We arrive at my apartment all too soon. Jack carries my bag in, kisses me softly, then turns to go. "I'll see you tomorrow?"

"Definitely." I melt into his embrace, cupping his face with my hand.

"I love you," he says softly.

"I love you too."

He kisses me one more time and then leaves with a smile that must mirror my own. Once

I close the door, I grab my bag and head to my room, unpacking everything and putting my dirty clothes in the laundry. When that's done, I look at my bed longingly and decide to take a nap. Lord knows I definitely didn't get enough sleep this weekend.

When I wake up an hour later, I reach over to my nightstand searching for my phone, but it's not here. Shit. Realization washes over me that it's still in my purse, turned off from our trip. I wander out to the living room, grab my phone, and set it down on the table to power up while I grab a glass of water in the kitchen. It buzzes several times, the vibrations humming against the table. Sipping on my water, I'm surprised to see I have dozens of texts from Gina, my parents, and several numbers I don't recognize.

I pull up Gina's texts first and my heart plummets as I read them. They're all from this morning.

Gina: Girl, what the hell did you do?

Gina: Did something happen with Jack?

Gina: I thought you weren't going to write the article that Vince wanted?!

I stop reading after that last one and call her. She answers immediately.

"Paige, what happened?"

I don't like the worry in her tone. "What are you talking about?"

"You don't know?"

"Know what?" My panic is starting to seep into my voice. "Gina, I've had my phone off

for the past few days. Jack and I went away to Malibu. What's going on?"

"Oh my God. This is so bad. You need to check out the *Chronicle* Sunday features section. I'll stay on the line while you find it."

I put my phone on speaker and then open my laptop and pull up the *LA Chronicle* website. I don't even have to find the Sunday features section because the featured article on the first page of the website has a picture of Jack front and center. The title taunts me, *NFL Star Quarterback, Jack Fuller, Opens Up,* but it's my name in the byline that makes me nauseous.

"What the hell?" I gasp. I start to skim the article and my heart plummets. "Oh my God. Oh my God."

"Paige?" I hear Gina call my name multiple times, but I've lost the ability to respond. I'm frozen staring at the screen, trying to absorb what I'm seeing in front of me.

"PAIGE!" Gina finally breaks through my brain freeze.

"Oh my God, Gina... I don't know how this even happened. This isn't my article. I never wrote this!"

"It's your name on the byline."

"I see that," I shout, panicking more by the minute. "Oh my God, Gina, Jack is going to see this." I'm horrified by the idea.

She sounds as defeated as I feel. "If he hasn't already."

"How did this even happen? How is this possible? There are things in here that I never put in my notes because I knew Vince could access the server if he really wanted to. How did he even get some of these details?" I'm shaking, frantically trying to figure out how this fucking happened.

"Gina, I have to go. I have to call Jack. I need to explain that I didn't do this."

"Call me back later, okay?"

I agree quickly, hang up, and immediately hit on Jack's contact info. It rings a dozen times before going to voicemail.

Shit, this is not good.

"Jack, it's me. I need you to call me back right away. Please, it's important," I plead.

I hang up and then call again. It only rings half a dozen times before I get his voicemail.

Did he just send me to voicemail?

The idea sits heavily in my stomach. Dread flows through my body as I attempt to call him again. When I get the same voicemail message, I decide to text him.

Me: Jack! Please answer your phone! I really need to talk to you.

When I see it's read, but no response comes, I send him another.

Me: Jack. If you saw the article, that wasn't me. I didn't write that. I don't know what's going on, but, please, you have to believe me! Please, call me.

I'm frantic with the desire to hear his voice. The pressure in my chest is overwhelming as I grasp the fact that everything is falling apart. A sob rips through my throat, and it's only then that I realize I'm crying. With trembling hands, I call Gina back.

"Hey, did you get ahold of him?"

"Gina…" My voice breaks and I can't keep the sob inside.

"Oh no, Paige. What happened?"

"He won't answer my calls or texts," I cry, feeling everything slipping away from me in

the blink of an eye. How did we go from having the most magical and perfect few days to this?

I curl up on my couch and cry, Gina trying to comfort me through the phone. Eventually, I tell her I need to go and hang up. I continue to attempt to reach out to Jack until midnight. My texts continue to go unanswered, and my heart breaks further when I notice that they are no longer getting marked as read.

I crawl under my covers around one in the morning and cry myself to sleep, feeling hopeless, frustrated, and overwhelmingly heartbroken.

THIRTY-EIGHT

Jack

I walk into my house on cloud nine from our weekend away, only to find Max sitting on my couch.

"Hey man, what's up?"

He looks at me with a mix of pity and guilt. "Jack, we need to talk. I think we read the situation wrong with Paige."

"What are you talking about?"

He fiddles with his tablet and then turns the screen to me. My heart plummets when I see a picture of myself on the screen with the title, *NFL Star Quarterback, Jack Fuller, Opens Up.* My eyes follow the title to the bolded byline, and my entire body stiffens in shock and betrayal.

"What the fuck?"

Max hangs his head, shaking it, before looking back up at me, remorse all over his features. "I'm so sorry, dude. I'm supposed to have your back, but I did not see this one coming. I really thought she was in this for real. If I had any idea this was what she was planning, I would've warned you, but everything seemed on the up and up with her."

I sink down on the couch next to him, reading the article filled with details about Paige and me. I notice there is a lot of personal shit we've talked about that she left out, and I'm grateful for that, but this is a complete betrayal that she wrote anything personal to begin with.

I'm surprised by how many details she included about our relationship, especially our past together. But most of all, I'm gutted that she would do this to me. She knows what my privacy means to me, and she didn't even talk to me about it. She promised she wouldn't do this. Did she know while we were in Malibu together that this article was coming out?

I feel like I just took a major hit and got the wind knocked out of me. How could Paige tell me she loved me when she knew she was going to do this? Was it really all a lie?

Dread fills my stomach at the thought.

My phone rings on the table, but I ignore it as I finish reading the article. It beeps with an alert and I glance down to see I have a missed call from Paige and a voicemail. When her smiling face lights up my screen as she calls me again, I can't help the bitter anger that flows through my veins. I click ignore and see that she leaves me another voicemail. Like I'm going to bother listening to any more of her lies. If she wanted to get back at me for breaking her heart in high school, mission fucking accomplished.

After a few more calls, she starts texting me. I open it.

Paige: Jack! Please answer your phone! I really need to talk to you.

Yeah, I'll bet, but I'm way too angry and betrayed to talk to her right now.

Paige: Jack. If you saw the article, that wasn't me. I didn't write that. I don't know what's going on,

***but, please, you have to believe me! Please,
call me.***

I scoff at her message. Wasn't her? Who the fuck else would know those details? I don't talk to any other journalists.

"Is that her?" Max asks.

"Yeah, she's trying to claim she didn't write it." I shake my head, my anger morphing to disappointment. I can't believe I let myself get played like this.

I can't believe Paige, of all people, did this to me.

"She's claiming she didn't write it? Who else would've written it?"

"No one but her. These details are too personal, although I suppose it was generous of her not to share everything."

"What do you mean?"

"I mean, I shared a lot more with her than this. More personal stuff that she could've easily written about. I'm a little surprised she included so many details about our relationship."

"Why do you say that?" Max asks, his tone hard to read.

I shrug. "I don't know. I've read a lot of her past articles when I was keeping tabs on her career. She never included personal stuff about herself or personal opinions in her pieces. I guess she was saving it for this. Fuck,"—I scrub my hands over my face—"I can't believe she played me like this."

I turn to Max, who's looking off into the distance with a confused, but thoughtful expression on his face.

"What?" I ask him.

He shakes his head. "I don't know. Just thinking."

"Well, I need a fucking drink." I get up and head to the kitchen. "You want one?" I shout.

"Yeah, I'll take a beer."

I grab two beers and move to the counter to grab the bottle opener. I set them down and brace my hands on the counter, my chin dropping to my chest.

God, this fucking hurts.

I try to take a deep breath, but I can't. I've only felt close to this one other time in my life and it was when I broke up with Paige. But her betrayal is adding a layer of pain that is unlike anything I've ever felt. I attempt one more deep breath, only mildly successful. I push off from the counter, open our beers, and then rejoin Max in the living room, passing him his drink as I sit heavily on the couch. He looks at me closely.

"What if she's telling the truth?" he asks cautiously.

I lie back against the couch and run my hand over my face, then roughly through my hair. "I don't know, man. I hate believing this was her, but the evidence kind of speaks for itself."

"But you said there were plenty of other personal details she didn't write about?"

"Yeah, so?"

"So, is it possible all of these details could've come from other sources?" he asks, pointing to the article still displayed on his tablet.

I shake my head. "I don't know, Max, and right now, I can't even think about it. I just want to get drunk and pass out." I'm overwhelmed by how shitty I feel, and I just want to drown my feelings. Not the healthiest reaction, but who fucking cares right now.

Not me. The only person I cared about just stabbed me in the goddamn back.

My phone beeps several more times.

"She keeps texting you."

I glance at the screen. Part of me is desperate to talk to her and hear her tell me she didn't do this. But the other, bigger, part of me can't bear to find out everything we shared was all a

bunch of bullshit so she could get an exclusive article and further her career. I pick up my phone and turn it off. I can't deal with this right now. I recognize that I'm shutting down, but it's the only thing I know how to do at this moment.

I pat Max on the back, offer him one of my guest rooms for the night, and then head up to my room. I fall back on my bed, staring up at the ceiling and wishing with every bone in my body that I could rewind to the past few days in Malibu and stay there forever. Instead, I'm here in my giant, empty fucking mansion in LA, heartbroken that the love of my life betrayed me and feeling like the life I thought I was going to have just got ripped away from me once again.

THIRTY-NINE

Paige

Marching into the office like a bat out of hell, I swipe a copy of the Sunday issue of the *Chronicle* off someone's desk as I make my way to Vince's office.

I woke up this morning with a rock in my gut, but that rock quickly morphed into fierce rage at Vince's backstabbing. He had to have gotten that information from somewhere, and I'm bound and determined to find out where.

I walk into Vince's office without waiting for an invitation and slam the paper on his desk.

"What the hell is this?"

He looks at me sardonically, then down at the paper. "Looks like your article."

"You and I both know I didn't write this trash. I'm going to ask you again. Who the fuck wrote this?" I demand, my voice getting louder with each word. I've already given up the idea of staying at the *Chronicle*, so at this point, I don't care if I'm being completely unprofessional. This man is the worst sort of editor imaginable, and I'd love nothing more than to rip him a new one.

Vince leans back in his chair, not a concern in the world.

"You and I both know you were never going to write the article I wanted. I had my suspicions weeks ago and put another reporter on it. She was to follow you and do whatever she needed to get enough information to publish a decently juicy feature story."

"Why did you put my name on the byline?"

Finally, he looks slightly uncomfortable but quickly covers it with his arrogance. "Alicia could only get information on your relationship, nothing personal about Jack. It would seem more believable and maintain our reputation if it was reported by the journalist in said relationship."

Alicia? What in the actual fuck? Suddenly all the times she appeared near me at work and tried to chitchat with me come back in stunning clarity. She was just trying to get close to me for this story.

"You have to write a redaction that this was written by someone else!"

"I don't have to do anything." He sneers.

"I didn't write this," I seethe.

"Prove it."

I'm literally about to explode, I'm so enraged in this moment.

"Fuck you, Vince. I quit."

I walk out of his office and go straight to the copy room. I open a box holding reams of paper, dump it out, and walk back to my desk with the empty box, quickly filling it with my few personal items.

A business card falls on the floor at my feet, catching my attention. I pick it up and look closer at the beautiful navy blue, embossed card. I remember the woman I talked to in the break-room last week, but I never paid attention to her name or who she was, too distracted by my Vince/Jack situation. The name on the card reads *Victoria Hunt*, and underneath, *Editor, News-worthy*. I tuck the card into my pocket, pick up my cardboard box and storm out, leaving behind the *LA Chronicle* and all the dreams that once came with it.

I get out to my car, and all my rage leaves me as if it's just been swept out to sea. I can no longer stop the onslaught of tears that have been waiting on the sidelines to make an appearance. The past twenty-four hours have wreaked havoc on my emotional state. I try calling Jack again, desperate to hear his voice. I need to know I can fix this, that I haven't lost him for good.

My heart breaks when it goes to voicemail on the fourth ring.

"Jack..." my voice cracks, but I push on, "Jack, I'm so sorry. I didn't write that article. I wish you would talk to me. Vince asked me to write a piece on you and I was trying to find a way around it. I was going to focus on your work with the high school and let you read it before I even presented it to Vince. I would never betray your trust and write anything personal about you, or us."

My heart is in my throat as I try to say as much as possible in the hopes that he'll finally understand and call me back. Right now, more than ever, I'm wishing I'd listened to Gina and told him about the article assignment to begin with. Then maybe we wouldn't be in this situation. But I let my fear get in the way, and now look where we are.

"Vince told me he put another reporter on it, and she wrote the article. They published it under my name so it would appear more believable." I scoff at that last part, so frustrated that Vince would do that. It's insanely unethical.

"Jack, I love you." My voice breaks, and a sob rips from my throat at the idea that I might never get to say those words to his face again if he won't forgive me. He's famous and powerful; he can easily keep me away from him forever.

"Please, Jack. I promise I didn't do this. I wouldn't do that to you. Please. Please, call me back," I plead. "I love you." I say those three words one last time and then hang up the phone.

I pull Victoria's card out of my pocket, staring at it and remembering our conversation. That day feels like a lifetime ago, but I can't forget her advice. I take a moment to pull myself together and then dial the number on the card.

"Victoria Hunt's office, this is her assistant Anna, how may I help you?"

"Hi, Anna, can you tell Victoria that Paige O'Malley called from the *LA Chronicle*. I'd really appreciate it if she could give me a call back." I leave my contact information and hang up.

I drive home, grateful that I brought my car to work this morning instead of walking. I manage to keep the tears at bay the whole way home, but the second I get into my apartment, I'm pummeled by the state of my life all over again. I slide down the front door and rest my head on my bent knees, feeling more defeated than ever.

"I have to fix this," I whisper to no one.

FORTY

Jack

The bright California sun lights up the conference room of the high-rise in downtown where I'm currently sitting as my agent, two PR reps, my lawyer, and Max all discuss ways to clean up this mess. Every sports reporter in the country, as well as other entertainment reporters, have been coming out of the woodwork in the hopes of getting a follow-up article. If only they knew that I never gave this one to begin with. I stare out the window while they discuss animatedly how we're going to get in front of the now-infamous *LA Chronicle* article and stop the other reporters from calling incessantly. I squint, thinking I can see Paige's apartment building from here, but the sharp ache in my chest reminds me that I shouldn't care about anything related to Paige right now. She's the reason I'm even sitting in this damn conference room.

"Hey, you okay?" Max whispers from next to me.

I turn to him and shake my head before looking down at my phone on the table in front of me. I spin it around with my finger, thinking about the voicemail that Paige left me just a bit ago. I haven't listened to it—I haven't listened to any of them—but it's longer than all her previous ones. I can't bring myself to hear her voice, especially if she's going to confess that she was behind this. I'm too afraid that she's calling to gloat that she finally broke my heart as badly as I broke hers in high school. Even though that's never really been Paige's style.

All my insecurities and fears from earlier in our relationship have reared their ugly heads and taken over. I know I'm being a coward by not listening to the voicemails, but I'm just not ready. Part of me feels like I deserve this for how I treated her all those years ago, but even that self-loathing doesn't ease the betrayal or the absolute ache in my heart from missing her.

I break away from my thoughts and heartache to hear my agent, Dan, agreeing with one of the publicists that we can definitely spin this as a good thing, while also making it clear this was a one-time thing.

He turns to me. "What do you think, Jack? Sound like a plan?"

I give him a blank look. I know I should care about what they've decided, but my heart's not in it. I turn to Max, knowing he's never led me wrong, and he nods his head. I turn back to Dan and the publicists.

"Sure."

The meeting wraps up fairly quickly after that, but I feel like I'm in a fog. As I separate from the group to walk to my car, I feel a presence behind me. I turn to see Max quickly catching up to me before I reach my car.

"Hey, I just wanted to check in with you to see if you need me to do anything."

I shrug. I don't really know what he wants from me right now, but I'm barely functioning and can't think past getting the fuck out of here.

"Seriously, Jack. I've never seen you like this. What can I do?"

I look up to the sky, letting out a hollow laugh at the situation I've found myself in. "You can't do a fucking thing." I turn toward my car but then turn back to him, catching him eyeing me cautiously. "You know the worst part?"

"What?"

"I don't regret a single minute with her. Maybe I deserved this for what I did to her a decade ago, but I wouldn't change these past few months with her." I take a deep breath. "Fuck, I even still love her." I shake my head, thinking that must make me the biggest idiot in the history of the world, but the heart wants what it wants, and my heart has always wanted Paige.

Max steps closer to me, his voice low and urgent. "Are you sure this was her? I've thought about it a lot and read that story a million times. The more I look at the situation, the less I think she wrote it. I even read a bunch of her old articles after the comments you made. It doesn't really sound like her. What if she's been telling you the truth in all those texts? Have you even listened to her voicemails?"

I look down at the ground and shake my head in shame. "I can't," I choke out.

"Why the fuck not?" He seems angry. Where the fuck does he get off being angry? I'm the one who got fucking screwed over.

"Because I can't bear to hear that she did it, okay!" I yell at him, angry that he doesn't seem to understand my hesitation. Angry that he's getting angry at me. Fuck, just simply angry at the whole goddamn mess.

He just stands there, shaking his head at me. "Dude, if she didn't write that story, then all you're doing is ruining the best thing you ever had." With that, he turns and walks to his own car.

His words haunt me for days, but I still can't bear to listen to her messages. With every day that passes, the dread in my stomach grows that he might just be right.

FORTY-ONE

Paige

My phone rings as I stare at my ceiling in a daze, while quiet tears stream down my splotchy cheeks. I snap out of my funk and quickly sit up to look at who's calling.

"Please let it be Jack," I whisper into the stagnant air of my apartment. I don't recognize the number, but that doesn't mean it's not him.

I answer with a hopeful, "Hello?"

"Is this Paige O'Malley?"

"Yes," I reply cautiously to the vaguely familiar female voice.

"Hi. It's Victoria Hunt, returning your call. Sorry it's taken me a few days to get back to you. Things have been a bit busy over here. Do you have a few minutes to chat?"

I quickly cover my disappointment that it's not Jack. "Yes, I do. Thank you for returning my call."

"Absolutely. Listen, I have to ask, especially after our conversation at the *Chronicle* a couple of weeks ago, did you write that article about Jack Fuller?"

"No. I didn't."

She hums knowingly. "Yeah, I didn't think so."

I'm surprised that she believed me so quickly. "You didn't?"

"Not at all. As soon as I read it, I knew it had to be a ghost-writer. After only a few minutes of talking to you, I knew that you'd never write about the man you told me about. His privacy was more sacred to you than a critical source's identity."

My heart hurts so much that Jack, who arguably knows me better than anyone, still believes I wrote it—if his silence is any indication—but this woman who only spent five minutes with me never believed for a minute that I wrote that article. I can barely breathe, so I just make an affirmative grunt that she's right.

"Jack knows you didn't write it, doesn't he?"

"Um..." I choke back the sob that wants to break out. I take a few deep breaths in an

attempt to compose myself. "I don't think so. He's not returned any of my calls." I mentally pat myself on the back for getting that out without my voice breaking.

"Oh, Paige. I'm so sorry."

"Actually, you might be able to help me."

"How?" I'm hopeful that she sounds so intrigued. "Well, I had this idea for an article..."

I wake abruptly to my phone buzzing. I see it's a text from Gina checking on me. The past four days have been absolutely miserable. I stopped trying to get ahold of Jack after my long voice-mail explaining the situation. I figured if I tried to call or text him anymore, he'd report me as some kind of stalker. The reality is if he wanted to talk to me, he would have. Clearly, he doesn't, and the pain that causes me is nearly unbearable.

The only thing getting me through my heartache is the

article I've been working on. I've barely slept between bouts of crying and obsessive writing.

It's been two days since my phone call with Victoria Hunt. She was impressed with my writing portfolio, but even more intrigued by the article I wanted to write to clear my name—and Jack's. She loved the idea I had and was happy to share it on her new online media platform called *Newsworthy*. Her phone call was the chance for redemption that I was desperate for.

Thinking about how positive and supportive Victoria has been motivates me to finish the final edits to the piece I've been toiling over. This has to be just right since it will most likely be my only chance to publicly clear the air and tell the truth. I print out the final copy, fold it carefully, and slide it into my purse. Next, the hard part.

I sit down gently on the stadium seat where I've sat so many times this season and look out onto the field. I spent extra time getting ready for this game because I haven't seen Jack in nearly a week, and I didn't want his first visual of me to be red, puffy eyes.

I'm wearing my favorite pair of dark-wash skinny jeans, black Rothy flats, and a cream blouse with polka dots and cap sleeves. It's a bit dressier than anything I would typically wear to a game, but I wanted to look good. My confidence in my relationship with Jack is very nearly depleted, and at this point I'm resigned to the fact that this is basically my personal Hail Mary pass.

The players run out to the field, and I see Jack's tall form instantly. My heart beats heavily in my chest being this close to him but still feeling like we're miles away from each other. God, what I wouldn't give to be able to touch him and kiss him right now. I miss him so fucking much.

He glances toward the seats and then does a double take. I hold my breath and sit up a little taller when his blue gaze settles on me. I'm bracing myself for the warmth that always accompanies his gaze, but I feel nothing but cold when he scowls and turns toward the field. He never looks back up at me.

As every second of the game passes without him looking at me, my heart sinks further.

My eyes never leave him while I silently beg *look at me*. It's not until I feel a tap on my shoulder that I finally avert my gaze, only for it to land on another familiar face.

"Max?" I can't help the hopefulness in my voice. Does this mean Jack wants to see me?

Max looks incredibly uncomfortable when he bends down next to my aisle seat. He leans toward me. "Paige, I'm here to ask you to leave."

I stare at him, my eyes wide and my jaw dropped, but my shock quickly morphs to pain. It's in this moment that my heart finally gives up on Jack, and I feel that loss in every fiber of my being.

Tears silently slip down my face, despite my useless attempts to stop them. This can't be happening. He never even gave me a chance to talk to him. Max's look turns sympathetic, which only adds to my misery. He clearly feels sorry for me.

God, how pathetic I must look.

My pain is quickly masked with anger.

I can't believe Jack's doing this. He seriously won't even fucking talk to me?

I look back out to the field, giving myself this last glimpse of Jack that I'll ever have. I grab my purse, stand up, and shove past Max, but turn back around because I just can't help myself.

"That's it, then?" The people around us look between Max and me, but I couldn't care less about them.

"I'm sorry, Paige. Really," he says sadly.

I shake my head and look up to the sky, attempting once again to stop the flow of my tears. My attempt is pointless as I make eye contact with him and feel them continue to slip down my cheeks.

"He's just giving up?" I shake my head. "God, I can't believe this. He's doing it all over again."

Max looks at me curiously. "Doing what?"

"Giving up on us without a fight," I reply sadly, defeat evident in every inch of my body. I'm done. There's no point trying anymore.

Why fight for someone who's not willing to fight for you?

"Goodbye, Max," I whisper.

I quickly walk away and out of the stadium as fast as I can. By the time I make it to my car, my tears have completely obliterated my makeup.

I always knew that if I gave Jack my heart again, I would never be the same. I just never thought it meant that I'd have to find a way to live without him again. This time, instead of merely breaking my heart, he's torn it out altogether.

FORTY-TWO

Jack

The football is clutched tight in my grip as I look for an opening. I know I need to pass the damn thing, but I can't see anything but a blur of bodies running around me. I don't know how to finish this play.

Fuck, I don't know how to do anything right now.

Suddenly I feel someone wrap their arms around me tightly, trying to pull me down to the ground. I fight with everything I have but feel like we're just working as counterweights for each other—neither of us reaching our goal successfully. I hear a whistle blow and the officials end the play, calling "in the grasp" —a call used to protect a quarterback from getting unnecessarily slammed to the ground and one they've not had to make for me for quite some time. I'm usually better than this.

I know I should be thankful the officials are trying to protect me, but I think I would've welcomed the pain of being slammed to the ground instead. Maybe it would finally ease this painful ache in my chest.

With every second that stretches on, I fight against the overwhelming urge to look back at the stands and see Paige. When I saw her before the game started, I was so frustrated with myself for not handling this situation right from the beginning that I couldn't stop the scowl from overwhelming my face. It wasn't until I turned back to the field that I felt the relief that flooded my body just from knowing she was here.

Over the past few days, I realized I was fucking things up, but I've still been struggling and couldn't pull my head out of my own ass. Seeing her today is the reminder I needed. She's too important to me to fuck this up anymore.

I've been distracted most of the game, trying to figure out ways to fix this mess I made. I couldn't bring myself to look at her again for fear that my body might actually betray me and take me straight toward her. Maybe I should've let that happen, because I've been playing like shit. I even noticed Max frowning at me before he left the field. I must really be sucking tonight if Max can't even stand to watch.

I continue playing like shit for the next half hour and feel my body sag with relief when we reach halftime. As we hustle off the field, I see Max back on the sidelines and shout his name to get his attention. I gesture for him to follow me, and he makes his way toward the tunnel leading to the locker rooms.

"What's up?" he asks when he finally reaches me.

"I need you to get a note to Paige. She's sitting in her usual seat."

He frowns at me and grips the back of his neck. "Actually, she's not."

"What do you mean?" My panic starts to rise.

"Dude, you were playing like shit. I saw you look at her at the beginning of the game and figured she was messing with your head. You've made it clear that you don't want to talk to her, so I made the decision to ask her to leave so you could focus on the game."

I shove him hard against the wall before my brain even registers what I'm doing. "You did what?!"

We're both surprised by my actions, but I don't release him. "You had no right to do that," I seethe.

His eyes are wide in shock, but his expression quickly morphs to an angry scowl as he puts his face right in mine. "Has something changed? Did you finally listen to her fucking messages? Because last I checked, you were being a fucking pussy. Excuse me for trying to protect the only thing you have going for you right now—your job!"

I stumble away from him and pace back and forth.

"Jack, you need to figure this shit out, man. You're a mess, and so is she."

That gets my attention. "What do you mean?"

I think back to my brief glance at her before the game started. She looked fucking beautiful as always. It nearly gutted me that she could look so put together while I've spent the last week feeling like a shell of a man.

"You're a fucking idiot, you know that?" he says angrily. "She was devastated to be asked to leave. Although weirdly enough, not all that surprised."

Fear prickles along my skin. "What do you mean by that?"

"She said something about how she shouldn't be surprised you were doing this—not fighting for her. She said you did this last time. You gave up without a fight."

He might as well have punched me in the gut for the effect his words have on me. Fuck. I did give up last time without a fight. And that's exactly what I've been doing, isn't it?

Why do I never fight for her when it matters?

Did I learn nothing from the last decade without her?

It's that last thought that nearly brings me to my knees. This is very different from last

time. If I lose her now, I'll never get her back.

I can't live without Paige.

I can't, and I won't.

"I don't care if she wrote that article or not, I want to be with her. I need to fix this." Max nods like he's been waiting a century for me to come to that conclusion.

The clearing of a throat interrupts us, and we both turn to see Matt Fischer standing there looking at us. "Sorry to interrupt, but Coach is looking for you, Jack."

Fuck, I wish this stupid game was over already. I need to get to Paige. I need to talk to her like I should have days ago.

I nod at Matt, and then we start heading into the locker room, leaving Max to go back out to the field. Matt stops me right as I reach for the doors. I look at him questioningly and am surprised by the guilty expression marring his face.

"I couldn't help but overhear what you and Max were talking about."

"Matt..." I go to stop him, but he quickly interrupts me.

"I think I was the source for that article," he says quietly.

"What?"

"I hooked up with some woman from that nightclub event we all attended. I was trashed,

and she kept asking questions about you and Paige. I didn't think anything of it."

I stare at him, thinking back to that night. He was wasted, I remember that clearly enough. I don't know what happened to him after I went to dance with Paige, but he overheard everything I shared with Max and Will. We all thought he'd be too drunk to remember anything the next morning. Clearly, we were wrong. I should've kept my mouth shut that night like I usually do.

My heart sinks further when he continues talking, and I realize with every word out of his mouth that I'm to blame for this article, not Paige.

Shit.

"Honestly, I figured she was just a jersey chaser looking to get in your pants and feeling out if you'd ever be available. I think I drunkenly told her some stuff about the two of you. Stuff you'd shared that night and things I'd heard in the locker room. I'm so sorry." He looks overwhelmed with grief and guilt for betraying a fellow player.

He continues, "I know this doesn't fix what I did. I read that article and felt sick to my stomach when I recalled sharing those things with the woman I met at the bar. She was gone before I woke up, and I never got her name. She said she was an office secretary, not a journalist. I know that's no excuse. I should've kept my mouth shut. Fuck, I should never have been as drunk as I was. I'm just so fucking sorry, Jack. I've been trying to tell you all week, but you've either been MIA or surrounded by other people. I didn't realize you and Paige had broken up over this, and now I feel even worse that I did this to you guys."

My brain is trying to absorb the information bomb he's just dropped on me. My body sags with relief while my heart drops to my stomach in despair. I'm relieved because this confirms that Paige wasn't behind this, but this also means I've royally fucked up, even worse than I already thought. I should've never doubted her in the first place. I'm way more at fault here than she is.

I need to fix this.

I pat Matt on the shoulder and forgive him because at this point, what's done is done, and it's clear he's been beating himself up over this. Besides, the realization that I'm the most to blame in this situation has changed my perspective.

The most important thing to do now is to make sure I can fix things with Paige. I head into the locker room with a vow to listen to her voicemails as soon as the game is over.

FORTY-THREE

Paige

Throwing my purse on the table, I walk into my apartment and slam the door behind me, wishing I could lock out the whole stupid world with that one gesture. I'm a strange mix of completely, utterly heartbroken and fiercely pissed off.

My phone rings, and I see Gina's name displayed.

"Hey," I answer.

"Oh shit," she whispers. "I'm guessing by your tone, it didn't go well."

"You guessed fucking right."

I lie down on my couch and stare up at the ceiling, defeat weighing me down like a fifty-ton weight. I give Gina the play-by-play of what happened at the game. She immediately gets angry on my behalf, and I almost laugh at hearing her rage about Jack having Max kick me out. She's one fierce friend, and I'm so grateful she's mine.

She must hear my heavy sigh because she asks, "What do you need? Want me to come down there and kick his ass? Or do you want to come up here and escape for a week or two? Hell, maybe we can get you a job back here, and we can be in the same city again."

I laugh at her excitement over that last suggestion. It feels good to laugh, even if it's short-lived. "I'm not quite ready to throw in the towel on LA just yet. I submitted my article to Victoria, and she's offered me a job."

"Really?! Damn, girl. I'm so proud of you, picking yourself right back up."

"Thanks."

"So what are you going to do about Jack?"

"I've done everything I can. I'm done." The agony of that sentence is damn near unbearable, but I fight the stinging in my eyes. I'm tired of crying. I'm tired of loving a man who clearly doesn't love me.

"I'm so sorry, Paige. I wish I could be there to hug you." Her warm, compassionate voice wraps around me like a blanket.

"I wish you were here too. Depending on my next assignment for Victoria, maybe I can come visit for a few days."

"You're welcome anytime. I'd love to see you."

"I'll let you know."

"So, what are you going to do now?"

I ponder her question as I stand up, walk toward my window, and look at the lights of

LA lighting up the darkness. "I think maybe I'm going to take Victoria's advice and focus on my career. Jack is going to be hard to get over, but I need to let him go, for good this time."

My heart rejects the idea completely, but I've decided I'm going to stop listening to it. It clearly has terrible self-preservation skills, and that's what I need now more than ever.

"Are you really ready to give up on him?"

"It doesn't matter if I'm ready or not. He's made it clear where we stand. I can't keep fighting for someone who doesn't want me. The rejection is too hard." My voice breaks, and the warm wetness falling down my cheeks only frustrates me further.

When will the tears finally stop? Why can't I be strong enough to hold myself together, especially after this last week? I mean, actions speak louder than words, and his silent treatment has been damn near deafening.

"Maybe you should block his number for a couple of days, give yourself time away from him."

"Not like it'll matter. He's not going to call me anyway." Still, I contemplate Gina's suggestion. Maybe it's not a bad idea. After all, I deserve more than this.

If Jack called me right now, would it be enough?

No. It definitely would not.

I take a deep cleansing breath, coming to terms with the fact that my heart will probably

always belong to Jack. "I'm going to focus on my new job at *Newsworthy*. It's got a lot more freedom than the *LA Chronicle* job, and it's still considered prestigious. It's a new era for journalism, and I get to be a part of it." My voice strengthens with determination. "My job can be my new love."

Gina and I talk for a few more minutes before we hang up. I glance down at my phone, and before I can rethink it, I scroll through my contacts. When I reach Jack's name, I open the contact info and hit the block button. I sigh, turn off my phone, and wait for the relief to come.

It doesn't.

I head to bed, my heart heavy but my determination strong. I will survive this pain. I will be strong enough.

Hopefully, if I keep telling myself that, I'll finally start to believe it.

FORTY-FOUR

Jack

I sit out on my patio, overlooking my pool and the view of Los Angeles as the sun rises. But the normally soothing view does nothing to ease the pain in my heart that only gets worse with every word I hear as I listen to voicemail after voicemail of Paige pleading for me to talk to her. Her last voicemail guts me, and I can't stop the tear that slides down my face when I realize what I've done. Her voice sounds more broken and defeated than any of the previous ones, but when it breaks at the end, that's when I cover my eyes and try my damnedest to reel in my emotions.

I can't cry right now. I need to fix this. I pull up her contact, needing to talk to her more than I need air to breathe. When I press call, it rings once and then goes straight to voicemail.

That's weird.

I try again. Same thing. It doesn't ring more than once, so I know she's not sending me to voicemail, and the call doesn't go straight to voicemail, so her phone must be on.

Did she block me?

My shoulders slump at the idea. In denial, I try calling her once more only to get the same result.

Fuck, I think she did.

My heart sinks. It's too little, too late. I need to do something bigger if I'm going to prove to her that I'm fighting for us. I don't care what it takes, because I'm going to win her back. There's no other possible alternative.

I can't live without her.

I hear Max shout my name from inside. "Out here," I holler back.

He walks out, takes in my haggard appearance, red-rimmed eyes, and the phone in my hand. "You listened to them." It's not a question.

"Yeah," I reply hoarsely.

"And?"

"I really fucked this up. I think she blocked my number."

He looks at me, curious. "Why do you think that?"

"Because I called her, and it rang once and then went straight to voicemail. All three

times."

His eyebrows shoot up in surprise. "Yeah, definitely sounds like she blocked you."

"I think I need to do something bigger."

"Uh, yeah, you'd be right about that. I'm guessing you haven't seen the latest."

"What do you mean?"

He fiddles with the tablet that I only now notice in his hand. "An article came out by Paige from a newer digital media source called *Newsworthy*. I just started following them in the last year. They're up and coming, but definitely getting some pretty incredible stories."

"Are we sure it's by her this time?"

"Oh yeah. She definitely wrote this one," he says as he hands it to me.

The LA Chronicle was my dream job. They are the largest print media source on the west coast. What journalist wouldn't dream of being a part of such a legacy? However, my dream quickly morphed into a nightmare when my editor manipulated me into agreeing to write an exposé on LA Wolves quarterback and NFL golden boy, Jack Fuller. My editor discovered that Jack and I had a history and used that to his advantage. My only option was to write the article myself to protect Jack.

With each passing minute, I realize Paige was trying to protect me all along, something she's doing even now when I least deserve it. My stomach rolls with nausea as shame overwhelms me.

I did not write the "scoop" printed in the Sunday features of the LA Chronicle last week. I never put myself in my published pieces, which can easily be confirmed by Googling any articles written by me in the past. This piece is the only exception to a professional rule of thumb that I have followed throughout my entire career, and I'm only doing it to clear the air.

Jack Fuller is one of the best people I've ever known. He's kind, generous, intelligent, and caring. He is also an incredibly talented football player, and the NFL is lucky to have him. He is passionate about his career and always gives his all on the field. At the end of the day, it shouldn't matter who he's dating, what he ate for lunch, or whether he wears boxers or briefs. All that should matter is that Fuller is a man of integrity, and he plays his heart out on the gridiron.

She's put it all out there, and I feel even more foolish for not trusting her.

I should've believed her from the very beginning.

I keep reading, unable to stop even though every moment that passes feels more painful than the last, as the weight of what I've done settles heavily on me.

I hope those of you out there who get a chance to read this article realize that the LA Chronicle *is no longer the prestigious news source it once claimed to be. It has fallen from grace most spectacularly, and I, for one, am thrilled that I no longer work there. They published an article under my name, about me, without my consent. By professional standards, that is highly unethical.*

The LA Chronicle *has proven itself to be untrustworthy and has gone from chasing legitimate stories to hunting for skeletons where there are none. Perhaps someday Jack Fuller will give a personal interview instead of just a professional one, but that choice should be his. In this case, it was taken from him, and for that, I will always be sorry.*

I finish the article and look up at Max. "I need to win her back."

"Fuck yeah, you do. You'll never find another woman who loves you like she does."

"I'm going to need your help."

"Done. What are we doing?"

I smile at my best friend. "I might have an idea, but I'll need you to do some things for me over the next couple of days, and then I need you to make sure she shows up to our game on Thursday night."

"I can do that."

We go over my plan, and Max agrees it's my best shot. I head off for practice, feeling more hopeful than I have all week. This has to work. But if it doesn't, I'm not going to give up. I'm never going to give up on Paige again.

FORTY-FIVE

Paige

I've been on a cleaning spree for the past couple of days in an attempt to keep myself from thinking about Jack. I've only been minorly successful on that front, but my apartment is spotless. I'm just finishing unloading clean dishes when my intercom buzzes.

I walk over to it and answer, "Yes?"

"I have a delivery for Paige O'Malley."

"Alright, come on up."

I buzz the front door to let the delivery man in. After signing for the medium-sized box, I move it to my kitchen table and open it up to see a bunch of small bundles wrapped with paper and bubble wrap. Each bundle appears to have a number on it.

I open the one labeled #1 first. I'm confused when I see a coffee cup. No one has given me a coffee cup to add to my collection for a while. I see the picture of the park Jack and I frequented a lot when we were dating in high school and take out the folded piece of paper tucked in the cup. My heart stops when I see Jack's familiar handwriting.

THIS WAS THE FIRST PLACE WHERE I FELL IN LOVE WITH YOU. I WAS YOUNG AND UNSURE OF MY FEELINGS UNTIL THAT SUMMER WHEN I CAME HOME FROM FOOTBALL CAMP AND YOU TOOK MY BREATH AWAY. YOU STILL DO.

I cover the sob that tries to escape as I read his words. I quickly open the second bundle to find another coffee cup, this one with a picture of the Chinook Point lighthouse. I pull out the slip of paper and read his words.

THIS WAS THE PLACE WHERE I MADE LOVE TO YOU FOR THE FIRST TIME. I'LL NEVER FORGET HOW GORGEOUS YOU LOOKED UNDERNEATH ME. I DIDN'T THINK ANYTHING COULD BE MORE PERFECT THAN BEING CONNECTED WITH YOU SO INTIMATELY. I STILL FEEL THAT WAY.

I place the slip back in the cup and quickly move to the third bundle, fighting the sting of tears in my eyes. This cup has a picture of the Point Fermin Lighthouse.

THIS WAS WHERE I KNEW WITHOUT A DOUBT THAT I STILL LOVED YOU. I KNEW I WAS DONE WAITING TO BE WITH YOU AGAIN BUT WANTED IT TO BE SPECIAL. I WISH I COULD'VE CAPTURED THE EXPRESSION ON YOUR FACE WHEN YOU DISCOVERED WHERE I'D TAKEN YOU. YOU LOOKED AT ME WITH SO MUCH LOVE IN YOUR EYES AND I DAMN NEAR SAID THE THREE WORDS THAT WERE CLAWING TO GET OUT. I STILL WANT TO SAY THEM.

My heart is beating profusely. He still loves me?

There are two more bundles. I quickly unwrap #4. It's a picture of the beach with the word Malibu written in a curly font near the bottom.

THIS WAS WHERE I FINALLY SAID I LOVE YOU FOR THE FIRST TIME SINCE WE GOT BACK TOGETHER. I'D BEEN FIGHTING THOSE WORDS SINCE THE FIRST MOMENT THAT I SAW YOU AT THE STADIUM. THOSE WERE THE MOST PERFECT FEW DAYS, AND A DREAM COME TRUE TO SPEND ALL THAT UNINTERRUPTED TIME WITH YOU, WAKING UP WITH YOU, LIVING WITH YOU, EVEN IF IT WAS ONLY TEMPORARILY. I STILL THINK THOSE WERE THE BEST DAYS OF MY LIFE SO FAR.

The final coffee cup has a picture of Sterez Stadium, where the Wolves play. Inside is a slip of paper and a ticket to the home game tomorrow night.

THIS IS WHERE I SAW YOU FOR THE FIRST TIME IN NINE YEARS AND REALIZED THAT YOU WOULD ALWAYS OWN MY HEART. IT'S STILL YOURS. ALWAYS. I'M SO SORRY FOR HOW I'VE TREATED YOU. PLEASE COME TO THE GAME TOMORROW.

I sink down into my kitchen chair and clutch the ticket to my chest.

He still loves me.

My heart is pounding, desperate to be reunited with him, but my mind is telling me to think this through. He broke my heart. He didn't trust me or believe in me, or us for that matter. He gave up on us.

Did he, though? My heart asks. *The display and words in front of you say otherwise.*

"Ugh, why couldn't he just have talked to me before? Why now?" I drop my head to the tabletop and groan my frustrations. I was finally accepting that he had given up and we were done.

Or at least I was getting there.

Okay, fine, I wasn't even close, but still.

Why does he get to blow me off for over a week and then

just turn around and get me crawling back to him? I hate this stupid situation and all the stress and heartache. I'm still feeling vulnerable from his last rejection.

I lift my head and stare at the ticket clutched in my hand. Is it enough? Can I forgive him that easily for giving up on us when I needed him to believe me? I take a deep, fortifying breath, hoping that I'm making the right choice.

FORTY-SIX

Jack

I pace back and forth in front of my cubby, waiting for Max to return. I haven't heard a word from Paige, but I know she got the delivery. I was notified when she signed for it and I've not been able to shake the nervous energy coursing through me all day. She has to show up. I need to know I didn't completely fuck this up with her.

"Hey, man, you doing okay?" I look up to see Will staring at me with concern marring his brow.

"I fucked up with Paige. You know that article that came out in the *Chronicle* a week and a half ago?" He nods. "Well, I thought she wrote it, but she didn't, and instead of even giving her a chance to tell me her side of things, I kinda blew her off."

Shame courses through my body as I think back on how I treated her. *Please let her come tonight. I need to see her.*

"I really hope you're able to work things out, man. What you two had seemed like the real deal. But if I were you, I'd be prepared to grovel hard. I have sisters, and if a guy ever treated them like that, I'd tell them to drop his ass."

I nod my head because I would expect no less from Will. But it also makes me a little sick that there's even a smidgen of a chance she won't let me fix this. Will leaves me to do his pregame ritual, while I sit on the bench, fidgeting with my hands and begging the universe to help me right this wrong.

"Jack."

I look up to see Max walk in and instantly shoot up from my sitting position. "Is she

here?"

He frowns apologetically and shakes his head. My heart sinks.

Fuck. She's not going to come.

"There's still time. The game hasn't even started yet," he attempts to reassure me.

I nod my head, but the reality is it doesn't matter if she comes to the game or not. I'm not letting her go, not this time. If she won't come to me, then I'll go to her.

Resolve and determination pump fiercely through my veins as I clap Max on the shoulder and then head out to the field. I need to come up with a Plan B. This time I'm not giving up without a fight.

FORTY-SEVEN

Paige

I chew on the inside of my lip as I watch the game start on TV. I debated getting in my car and using that ticket a million times, but I just couldn't do it. At the end of the day, I need Jack to do more than send me coffee mugs and notes—as much as his words mean to me. It's just not enough after the week and a half he's put me through. After once again not fighting for us and worse, choosing not to trust me, or even giving me a chance to explain.

With a groan of frustration and an ache in my heart, I click off the TV at the first mention of Jack's name. I don't know why I'm torturing myself anyway. I wonder what he'll think when he realizes that I'm not coming to the game.

That's another thing that hurts—that he thought I'd so easily come to his game after my last experience at that stadium. Yeah, no thanks.

I bustle around my small apartment, searching aimlessly for something to take my mind off Jack and the ticket still sitting in a coffee mug on my kitchen table, taunting me from afar.

I pick up my e-reader and attempt to read the romance I started reading before everything fell apart with Jack, but my brain keeps wandering. After reading the same paragraph half a dozen times, I toss it aside and let out a heavy sigh. I reorganize the magazines on my coffee table and then decide to reorganize my kitchen cabinets. It's mindless work, but at least I'll feel productive afterward. Connecting my phone to my Bluetooth speakers, I find my favorite playlist and start working.

I've completed reorganizing most of my cupboards when my phone rings. My heart stalls for a moment before pounding furiously as I rush over to it wondering if it's Jack calling.

Gina's name flashes on the screen and I don't bother hiding my disappointment since there's no one else around anyway. Of course it's not Jack. He's playing a football game right now.

"Hey," I say.

"Hey, lady. How're you doing?"

I shrug even though she can't see me. "Eh, I've been better."

"Are you regretting your decision?" Gina is the only person who knows about his attempt to smooth things over and about the ticket he sent me to come to tonight's game.

"Not regretting it, but wishing things were different." I sigh heavily, fighting back my emotions as they pummel me one by one. "I wish he'd listened to me in the first place. I wish he'd known me well enough to give me the benefit of the doubt. I don't know what ultimately changed his mind—whether he finally realized what we had was worth fighting for, or he read my article—but it all feels too little, too late.

"He's never fought for us, Gina. He gave up when we were teens, and he did it again as soon as the going got tough. I don't think I can go through that again."

"What would it take for him to fix it?"

I stare aimlessly at the wall in front of me, my eyes glassy with unshed tears. "I don't know. But more than coffee cups and a ticket to his game, that's for damn sure."

"I'm so sorry, Paige. I wish there was something I could do."

"Me too," I reply, my voice hoarse from all the emotion that I'm barely holding back. "You know what really sucks?"

"What?"

"I think he was the one. Hell, I've always thought that, even after he broke my heart. But maybe not everyone is destined to get a happily ever after."

"You're still gonna get yours. It'll happen. For all you know, the right guy could come banging down your door in no time."

"Yeah, maybe. But maybe I should just take a break. Focus on my career and determine if LA is the right place for me. It's not gonna be easy seeing Jack's name and face everywhere."

"True, but you're strong enough to handle whatever life throws your way."

"Thanks, Gina. I'm going to drink a giant glass of wine, veg out in front of the TV, and then head to bed. I'll talk to you later, okay?"

"Sounds good. Night."

I end the call, still feeling as melancholy as ever. Looking around, at least my apartment is clean and my kitchen cabinets are all neatly organized. Now if only my emotions could be tidied up that easily.

After pouring myself a giant glass of wine—and then choosing just to bring the bottle with me—I sit down on my couch and turn on the TV.

The football announcers mock me with their play-by-play of the last touchdown. There's no mention of Jack, but they do mention the backup quarterback multiple times.

Is Jack not playing?

Did he get hurt?

I try to tamp down my worry over his well-being. He's not mine to worry about anymore. That thought only brings the tears I've been fighting back closer to the surface, until one finally breaks free and slides down my cheek. I try desperately to pull myself together, but it's like I've held it in for so long that now everything is exploding out of me uncontrollably.

I barely hear the knock at my door through my sobs, but once I do, I quickly run to the kitchen, splash some water on my face, and then make my way to the door. I don't know who it could be at this time of night since my neighbors mostly keep to themselves and I'm not expecting anyone. Maybe Gina sent me something to try to cheer me up. That would be just like her.

I peek through the peephole and inhale a sharp breath before opening my door and letting my hungry gaze linger on his body before my eyes meet his.

"Jack."

FORTY-EIGHT

Jack

It's hard to breathe as I stare into the red-rimmed eyes of the woman I love more than anything else in this world. The evidence that she's been crying guts me and nearly sends me to my knees. I knew I fucked up, but seeing it—actually *seeing* how much I hurt her—kills me.

"What are you doing here? Why aren't you at your game?"

I know I have limited time before she shuts that door in my face, so I don't dillydally.

"I had to see you. As soon as I realized you weren't coming to the game, I told Coach I couldn't play tonight and headed straight here." I take a quick measured breath and then say, "Paige, I'm so fucking sorry. I never should've doubted you." My voice breaks at the end because I'm not entirely sure it's enough, but I'll do whatever it takes for her to forgive me. I can't lose her, not again.

She stares at me like she's not sure if I'm real or not before her eyes turn cautious and she asks, "Why did you?"

"I don't know if I can explain it very well."

"Try," she whispers.

I know it's the least I can do, so I try to put into words why I monumentally screwed this up. "When we first got back together, you seemed hesitant about what was more important to you—your career or me. I knew you worked your ass off to get to the *Chronicle*, and for a while, I wasn't sure if that meant you'd sacrifice us to solidify your place at the paper. Then, Max mentioned that he'd turned you away from the stadium one day because you were snooping around for a story."

"I wasn't—"

"Paige," I cut her off, "please, let me get this out. Okay?"

She nibbles on the inside of her lip but remains quiet, so I continue. "He and I agreed that it didn't seem like that was your intention in dating me, but it planted more doubt in my mind about us." I take a breath. "Then we had those amazing three days in Malibu, and I'd never felt more secure in our relationship. We were strong. I loved you and I believed you loved me. And then when I got home and found out about the article, it felt like I got sacked and couldn't breathe."

She opens her mouth to speak, but I put a finger against her lips. "I'm not done. You'll get your turn, I promise, but I've been silent for too long."

She huffs out a breath but remains silent.

"Max questioned the authorship of the article almost immediately. I wish I could say I did as well. I'm ashamed that I doubted you, but as soon as I saw your name attached to that article, I questioned everything. I was so lost in my doubts that I felt frozen. I couldn't do anything but go through the motions."

"So, what changed?"

"You showed up at that game the other day and I was overwhelmed by how good it felt to see you. It was like a huge weight was lifted and I realized how stupid I'd been to not give you a chance to explain.

"But you sent Max to make me leave." I can hear the hurt in her voice and it damn near kills me.

"No, I didn't," I say emphatically. "He did that on his own, and trust me when I say I ripped him a new one for it when I found out what he did. That was about the same time he called me out for being a pussy and not listening to your voicemails."

"You never listened to any of them?"

I shake my head, watching her absorb this information. "I couldn't. Not until that night. Then I listened to all of them, and hearing those on top of Matt's confession made me feel like the biggest piece of shit for how I'd treated you."

"Matt's confession? Who's Matt?"

"Matt Fischer is a tight end on the team. He got super wasted at that club night and apparently hooked up with some chick who kept asking about you and me. He thought she was just a jersey chaser looking to score if I was available."

"Gross." She shivers like she's repulsed by the idea, and I can't help the smirk that appears on my face.

"Yeah, well, we've all made mistakes. Regardless, he felt pretty bad and spilled everything. He recognized some of the details that were in that article. He didn't know she was a reporter until the story came out."

Paige looks off to the side and nods like she's putting something together. "It must've been Alicia. That's who Vince sent to get a juicier story since I refused."

"Paige, I'm so sorry. I can't say it enough. Please tell me it's not too late for us. I can't lose you. Not again. I gave you up once, and I've regretted it ever since. I've lived the last nine years feeling like something was missing."

"I know the feeling." She looks up at me, fresh tears glistening in her eyes.

"I can't go back to life without you," I whisper, my heart in my throat, because I know I'll be a shell of a man for the rest of my life if I can't fix this. "I love you so fucking much. You're still my best friend, Paige. You're still my everything."

I look into her eyes, silently pleading for her to remember the first time I whispered almost those exact same words. We were heading toward a crossroads in our relationship, and we ended up making the wrong choice. Well, *I* made the wrong choice for us. I don't want to look back on my life ten years from now wishing I'd done something different.

"I'm not giving up this time. I'll do whatever it takes, but I won't give up. Ever. What'll it take, Paige? Tell me, and I'll do it. Please," I beg. Fuck, I'd get on my knees right now and beg if I thought it would help my chances.

"I need you to believe me next time," she speaks softly, reaching a hand out and cupping my face.

"Next time?" My question betrays my hope that she's saying we're going to be okay.

She nods. "I love you, Jack. With my whole heart. It's always been you. It will always be you."

She goes to say something more, but I can't help myself. I need to touch her, to be connected with her. I kiss her soft, luscious lips, desperate to taste her.

She breaks from the kiss. "I'm so sorry about the article in the *Chronicle*. I seriously had no idea Vince would be such a backstabbing asshole."

I kiss her again, over and over. I kiss her cheeks, her forehead, her nose. All the while, she continues to try to apologize.

"Stop." I look her boldly in the eyes. "You have nothing to apologize for. I was the asshole in this situation. All I want is to move forward. With you. Can we do that?"

She nods her head enthusiastically, a smile breaking out on her gorgeous face. "Yes!"

She kisses me passionately, and for the first time in almost two weeks, my whole body feels calm and centered. This, right here, is where I belong.

Paige

EPILOGUE

One Year Later - Christmas Eve

"Mom, seriously, you don't have to help. You're supposed to be relaxing and enjoying your vacation." I chastise my mom for the fourth time in the last half hour. My parents are visiting from Chicago for Christmas. Jack's parents are also visiting from Portland. They've been having a great time catching up.

"Oh, honey, I know I don't have to. I want to." She smiles at me lovingly, and I give in. I've been cooking most of the day trying to make a Christmas Eve feast for our first joint family holiday.

"Paige, I love what you've done with this house. When Jack lived here by himself, it seemed so empty."

"Oh, thank you, Mrs. Fuller, but really, a lot of it was just things we found on trips or exploring the city together. It was really a joint effort to make it a little bit homier."

"Paige, how many times do I need to tell you to call me Claire?"

I blush. I'm still adjusting to calling Jack's parents by their first names. When I was little, my parents made sure I was always polite with them and respectful. That meant calling them Mr. and Mrs. Fuller. Now that Jack and I have been dating for over a year, they're determined to make me drop the formality. Unfortunately, it's been a hard habit to break.

Three months after Jack and I worked through all the *LA Chronicle* drama, he asked me to move in with him. He said he would've asked me sooner but didn't want to spook me. Fortunately for him, spooked was the last thing I was feeling when he asked me.

The past year with Jack has been the best year of my life. Our relationship is so much deeper than it was when we were kids and teens. We've developed a comfort and intimacy that makes me feel so safe and secure, while at the same time, the passion between us is practically combustible.

"Hey, babe,"—Jack leans down and kisses my hair when he enters the kitchen—"it smells great in here."

"Thanks. It's almost done. I'm just finishing the potatoes. My mom is about to pull out the green bean casserole and then we should be good to go. Can you grab the drinks for the table?"

"Sure thing. Need anything else?"

I look around the kitchen and out to the table that is already covered with dishes of food. "Nope, I think that's it."

"Okay." He smiles at me and then kisses me quickly before winking at me and walking toward the fully stocked bar next to the dining room area.

He's been very affectionate today. Not that he isn't normally affectionate, but he's not usually quite so obvious about it when we're around our parents.

Dinner is a huge success. I feel like I spend most of it blushing from all the compliments over the food. I love cooking, something I really started enjoying once I got to use Jack's dream of a kitchen—well, now *our* dream of a kitchen. After hours of visiting while letting our food digest, Jack interrupts the several different conversations going on around the table.

"I think it's time for presents," he says loudly and confidently.

With murmurs of agreement, we all make our way into the living room where we've put up a massive Christmas tree, decorated with white and multicolored twinkle lights. It was a beast to get into the house, but it's gorgeous, and I love the fresh pine smell.

Jack passes out the presents, and we take turns opening them. I go to open my big present when Jack stops me.

"Open that one last," he says, his eyes twinkling.

Shrugging, I concede and open a smaller present. It's an absolutely beautiful leather-covered photo album, but when I open it, I notice it doesn't have pictures in it.

"My recipes! Oh my God, Jack, this is perfect! Thank you!"

"You mentioned you wanted a book to put them in, and you'd already written a bunch on those recipe cards you bought. There's plenty of space in there to add more."

"I love it. Thank you so much, babe." I kiss him quickly, already excited to add more recipes to this book.

Everyone opens the rest of their presents, and then my big one is the last one left.

"I wonder what it could be," I say jokingly to the group. I'm sure something this big is either for my home office or the kitchen since those are the two places I use the most.

I tear off the wrapping and open the box to find a slightly smaller box inside. I pull it out and unwrap it, only to find another smaller box inside. I laugh and look at Jack.

"Is there even a present in here, or are you just messing with me?"

"There's a present. Keep going."

I smile at him and resume opening the present. I keep laughing when each box holds a

subsequent smaller box until I'm surrounded by wrapping paper and varying sizes of cardboard boxes.

"Okay, seriously. You're messing with me, aren't you?" I laugh but continue to open the box. My laughter dies in my throat as I pull out the coffee cup with a small black velvet box in it.

I look up at Jack and find his eyes are already on mine, shining with so much love it makes me breathless.

"Open it," he whispers.

With shaky hands, I open the black velvet box to see the most beautiful, brilliant round cut diamond engagement ring in a platinum setting.

"Jack," I whisper. I look up just in time to see him drop down on one knee as he carefully grabs the box out of my hand.

"When I was five years old, I met this girl who became my best friend. When I was sixteen, she transformed my world completely by loving me. I was dumb enough to let her go once, but I'm never going to make that mistake again.

"Paige, I've loved you practically all my life, even when you weren't in it. You were always here," he vows as he points to his heart. "You never left, not once. I've never loved anyone the way I love you. You're my best friend, my everything. Always. Will you marry me?"

Tears stream down my face as I emphatically nod my head and whisper "Yes" over and over. I watch with an unprecedented joy as he takes the ring out of the box and slides it onto my left ring finger. The second it's fully seated at the base of my finger, I grab his face with both my hands and bring his lips to mine.

My heart is filled with happiness as we smile and fight

joyful tears surrounded by our parents. I kiss Jack again and as he looks deeply into my eyes, I know only one undeniable truth.

This man is mine. Always and forever.

Thank you so much for reading *In the Grasp*. Will and Gina's story is available now where all ebooks are sold. Grab your copy today!

Want to read Max's story? Subscribe to my newsletter to get his novella delivered straight to your email.

AFTERWORD

If you enjoyed this book, I would be forever grateful if you would leave a review.

Being an indie author can be really exhausting because you do so much of this business by yourself, but I feel really fortunate to have found some incredible people to help me make my books what they are.

To Ann and Ann, I can't even begin to put into words how grateful I am to have found you. You've made my books so much stronger. Thank you for being the best editors a girl could've asked for.

To Kate Farlow, who designed all the covers for this series. You have been a huge blessing. Thank you for creating such gorgeous and drool-worthy covers (and finding all those sexy abs!).

To Daphne, Kenna, Kelly, and Ellie. I seriously don't know what I'd do without you ladies. I'm so grateful we found each other. Thank you for talking me off the ledge whenever imposter syndrome strikes.

I also need to thank Amy Daws. She's been such a huge inspiration to me, and I've loved her as an author for years.

When I finally finished the first draft of this novel and decided I wanted to pursue self-publishing, she pointed me in the right direction (she probably doesn't even know this), and I will be forever grateful for that simple piece of guidance.

To my best friend, Rikki, thank you for being the best beta reader and sounding board in the world. I don't know what I would do without you. I owe you an epic dance party the next time we get to see each other. "You gotta be bold..."

To my husband, you are my rock. Thank you for putting up with my crazy antics and messiness. I love you the most.

To my sweet baby boy, thank you for being the wonderful miracle you are. You make every day such a gift and I can't wait to watch you chase your own dreams.

To my mom for coming over and babysitting when I was up against a deadline and really needed to hide in my writing cave to get it all done. You're the best and I feel so blessed to be your daughter.

And to you, the reader. Thank you for picking up my book and giving it a shot. I know you have millions of amazing authors to choose from and I'm honored you read my words. I hope you enjoyed them!

ABOUT THE AUTHOR

Cadence Keys writes steamy contemporary romance novels full of heart, heat, and HEAs. She loves football (especially seeing all those tight ends), coffee (it sustains her), and watching Gilmore Girl marathons (witty banter for the win). When she's not busy writing, she's spending time with her family or getting lost in a good book (always romance).

You can also find more information about all future releases at www.cadencekeysauthor.com/

facebook.com/cadencekeysauthor
twitter.com/cadencewrites
instagram.com/cadencekeysauthor
bookbub.com/profile/cadence-keys
goodreads.com/cadencekeysauthor